TH CRAZIEST BOOK EVER WRITTEN

a novel

Mr. W.

MONTAG

Montag Press ISBN: 978-1-957010-43-4
Design © 2024 Amit Dey

Montag Press Team:

Cover: Rick Febre
Editor: Charlie Franco
Managing Director: Charlie Franco

A Montag Press Book
www.montagpress.com
Montag Press
777 Morton Street, Unit B
San Francisco CA 94129 USA

Montag Press, the burning book with the hatchet cover, the skewed word mark and the portrayal of the long-suffering fireman mascot are trademarks of Montag Press.

Printed & Digitally Originated in the United States of America
10 9 8 7 6 5 4 3 2 1

DEDICATION

To all the writers who torment their characters the way God torments the poor and sick.

ACKNOWLEDGEMENTS

This book was born from the dream that took place in the middle of Bright Monday night. A barefoot woman in a red cloak confronted me in the forest. Far behind her was an angry mob with torches, forks, and spikes heading forward. She told me they were the characters from my books who wanted to kill me. They were angry because I didn't write about them. She shook me like an earthquake saying that I needed to write. I woke up and started writing straight away. Therefore, I would like to acknowledge the unknown forces behind my dream and express my sincere gratitude for their doing.

Of course, nothing would be possible without publishers, editors, readers, and many other individuals who comprise and contribute to this puny civilization. Instead of writing their names, I chose to give big thanks to all mothers and fathers for having unprotected sex and suppress my doubts that it might have been a bad idea.

1

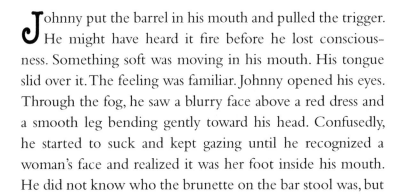

Johnny put the barrel in his mouth and pulled the trigger. He might have heard it fire before he lost consciousness. Something soft was moving in his mouth. His tongue slid over it. The feeling was familiar. Johnny opened his eyes. Through the fog, he saw a blurry face above a red dress and a smooth leg bending gently toward his head. Confusedly, he started to suck and kept gazing until he recognized a woman's face and realized it was her foot inside his mouth. He did not know who the brunette on the bar stool was, but she seemed familiar. Johnny tried to make space for words.

"It backfired," the brunette said as she shoved her foot deeper. Her toes bashed his throat and pushed the back of his head onto the bottom of the sofa. "You could have at least left some message… But then again, you have written so many books no one cared to read. Besides Lara… But she doesn't count. Why would it be any different with a goodbye letter…"

His neck hurt like hell, his body sprawled over the floor, and his legs spread over the upturned table. Next to it, little pieces of glass jutted from a puddle of whiskey. Johnny was grunting. He clutched her slender ankle with both hands in an attempt to push it out but was too weak. She pushed her leg further and her heel almost slipped in. Johnny was choking while her foot bathed in his saliva deep in his mouth.

"I thought you were going to like this." She smiled with a raunchy look in her eyes. Shadows and dark lights danced over her face. Then she stopped, held still for a moment, and pulled her foot out. A line of saliva hung between his mouth and her toes before it snapped and fell on his chin. Her feet went below his balls.

"Who are you?" Johnny mumbled.

"Are you saying that you don't recall?" The brunette swayed her legs up and her beautiful feet emerged above that pretty face. She slid her dress from her thighs, revealing a peachy cunt. Then she lowered her legs to a rope, her soles dangling in the air. Finally, the mysterious beauty crossed her legs and put her wet foot back on top of his balls. "Nothing? Seriously? All right… It's me… Joana…"

Johnny frowned.

"Nothing?" A sour smile swallowed her face. "The woman the Grimm brothers would call 'all in one'? Come on. Cinderella and Red Riding Hood."

Johnny's lips parted as he stared at her while he tried to get up.

"I hope you recognize me now," she said.

"It can't be."

"Plotting with the wolf to kill the granny because of her will, and to overtake the kingdom. Yes, it can be! It is me!"

"No! This must be some kind of joke," Johnny said as he stumbled onto the sofa and fell on his back. Then, just as suddenly, he jumped back to his feet and approached Joana.

"If you think of your books as jokes, then sure... They are a bit bizarre. I never understood them myself. I even wondered a few times, am I some kind of joke?" she said, looking at him inquiringly.

As she spoke, Johnny slid his fingertips over Joana's face. Warm and gentle like Saharan sand with barely visible freckles scattered over her cheekbones the color of chocolate. Sharp green eyes of everlasting spring. His thumb slipped inside her lips and touched the scar on her jaw. Johnny jumped back and almost fell over the sofa again.

"Calm down! Everything is all right."

"I must be going insane!" He jumped, running his fingers through his hair, dark and thick, like the confusion devouring his mind.

"You are not insane."

"Yes, I am! I must!" His face twitched as his gaze swirled over the room. Like a sinking ship, the room swayed with every step Johnny made. "I've had enough! No more! Where is my fucking gun? I am over with this shit! Where is my gun?"

"Stop shouting!" Joana opposed. "It is in a safe place where your hands can't reach it."

"Give me my gun! I have had enough of this fucking life! I want to end it! Right away!"

"I too have had enough of my life. Why do you think I am here? But at least you can go kill yourself."

"Enough!" Johnny shouted and smashed a vase that he had picked from the tiny kitchen, glass flying all around. "All right! No gun! It will be the bridge!" he roared as he strode out of the door into the night. Joana rushed after him.

He stumbled over bags full of garbage and flattened grass. Getting back to his feet, he rushed forward. A skinny black dog stood in his path, barking. Joana was yelling for him to stop, but the writer didn't even notice when the dog squealed and retreated to avoid Johnny's fat sole squashing his paw. Along the dusty road cutting through the desolate outskirts, he rushed toward the bridge.

Connecting two naked hilltops above a raging river stood the mighty bridge made of iron and stone. Under the full moon, barely glimpsed between the foggy clouds, it resembled a blurry black line some child had clumsily pulled to link a pair of dots on paper.

The streetlights were far away from each other, and every second lamp was broken. That meant Johnny could dive into the shadows every twenty yards, disappear, and then reappear in the glow of the next light he was approaching. In one of those ventures, halfway to the bridge, a big man in a long gray coat rushed out of the blackness and crashed into Johnny. The writer froze as the big tall guy with an enormous black hat and furrowed face gripped his jacket with both hands and pushed him forward.

"I demand life!" the big man boomed.

"Who are you?" Johnny whimpered, trying to free himself.

But his grip was too strong. The man lifted his head so the writer could see his white eye without a pupil and the little tattoo of a black rose sprawling on his cheek below.

"This can't be!" the writer said, barely catching his breath. But it seemed it could be: he was the nameless executioner from "Saharan Maze."

"I demand to live!" the man repeated. His hands in leather gloves released Johnny's jacket and cupped his face. The writer felt the increasing pressure over his skull and tried to push himself away. But he could not move an inch. The big man was as solid as stone, just as he should be.

"Let go of me!" Johnny shouted, his head boiling.

The man pushed him. Johnny flew back and painfully groaned when his back and head hit the concrete. Lying there, the writer's blurry gaze faced up to the clouds. His heart was beating like it intended to pierce its way through his chest. When Johnny propped himself on his elbows, the big man was gone. Only red petals whirling in the wind remained. And the fading sound of bleating coming from the darkness.

When he got to his feet, he was panting. The bridge was still a ways and there were many broken lamps ahead. He proceeded, looking over his shoulder every few steps.

Getting closer, the bridge was getting bigger. Johnny could see the stairs leading up to the railings from which he planned to surrender to gravity. The river would do the rest. He read somewhere that water is as hard as concrete if you jump properly. Even if you don't, the river was deep and cold in fall and the current was always fast.

As he was passing a working streetlight, a black cat crossed his way. He chuckled, remembering how he had read that black cats are the only animals that suffered a genocide when people in the Middle Ages believed they were to be blamed for all misfortunes. As the cat disappeared into the dark, Johnny felt a touch on his shoulder. He screamed, jumped, and turned around.

"Forgive me." The words came from an old lady in a black dress and a big hump on her back. "I didn't mean to startle you."

"It's all right," he said in disbelief. "Isn't it a bit late for you to be outside?"

"Late for me, early for you," she replied. "I don't get it. Why would a man who decided to kill himself fear anything?"

Johnny stepped back. "Who are you?"

"You never named me," she answered. "And I am not here because I want to live. Being an ugly old lady with a side role is not much of a life to lose. But you gave me a beautiful granddaughter. I am here because of her."

"What is going on?" Johnny shouted, waving his hands over his head.

"I just don't want you to torture her much. And I want you to give her a happy ever after. Please. You don't need more than a day," the old lady begged.

"I am done," Johnny hissed, turned, and rushed towards the bridge.

"Go ahead, you selfish bastard! I hope Dominic gets hold of you and gives you what you deserve before the end!" she shrieked.

Johnny's heart jumped. He froze. Then he turned around timidly. But there was no trace of her.

"What the hell!" he hissed through his teeth. The bridge was not far. As soon as he started walking, Johnny heard murmuring. But he did not dare to turn around. His entire body shuddered and his legs started running on their own.

2

The writer had to climb a lot of stairs to the top. He was panting like a dog and white steam from his mouth danced before his face. Yet, the fatigue of his body didn't soften the rage of his soul. The world's suffering echoed in his mind in answer to the question of how a man who decided to die feared anything.

The murmuring was gone, but he had the feeling of being followed. The cuboidal spiral concrete stairs prevented him from seeing what was below and he sure as hell was not going to wait. This was his night. He was determined to put a full stop to the script he was being forced to live.

As he reached the top, Johnny flipped his middle fingers toward the sky. He could not hold out for long. He leaned forward as his arms fell to his bended knees. It takes time for a smoker to catch his breath after so many stairs. When he could breathe normally again, the writer raised his arms and again flipped both middle fingers towards the sky.

"For you!" he screamed. "And your beautiful son! And that bloody Mary! Or whatever her name really is! You wouldn't even let the gun kill me! And now you go and fuck with my brain! To lock me in an asylum! Well, I have news for you, Daddy! Not gonna happen!"

The writer strode to the middle of the bridge. He wanted to make sure his body didn't hit any of the concrete. If he did, Johnny feared he would miraculously survive and spend the rest of his life as a plant. He was going to jump into the river on his stomach, hoping the clash with the water would kill him. And if not, he will let himself drown. He had robust leather shoes, sturdy jeans, and a red sweater under his leather jacket. When all that gets soaked, it will be: Goodbye, Johnny, the writer thought as he leaned over his hands on the fence.

One last time, he looked towards his old trailer, muffled light pouring out from the window, a few black blurs: Shadows… Someone was already in. Johnny smiled at how poor the souls inside were if they found something of value. And for a moment he thought of Joana and hoped they didn't hurt her: if she was real at all. It would be a shame for a lady with such beautiful feet to suffer.

The writer's gaze swept peacefully over the road winding through the desolate area with a few scattered houses and other trailers with dim lights peeking out through the curtains. Somewhere in the middle, he spotted two small red dots next to each other. They began blinking and widening until they took the shape of ellipses. Johnny realized those were eyes: a pair of red eyes looking straight at him from the shadows beneath the broken bulbs. The lights extinguished one by one, the red blurs moving like the wind, Johnny's heart started to bang.

"Dominic," he mumbled, feeling his spine turning into an icy spike.

The writer's body trembled. The red gaze was now under the stairs. He heard the murmuring. There was no time for goodbyes or thoughts. Johnny threw one leg over the railings. Then the other one. Balancing his heels on the little ledge, he turned so that his belly was facing the water.

A song sounded. It was jazz: Cantina. Then the loud sound of an engine, followed by the rumbling of tires and bright headlights blinded his eyes. Johnny didn't want to look away. He let go. But someone had already grabbed him. The firm grip lifted his body, dragged him over the railings, and shoved him into the trunk of what looked like a black Bentley.

The trunk was tiny and soft, as if enwrapped in sponges. Something was moving inside. Thin like a rope, slithering and hissing. It was a snake, the writer realized with terror. A black, almost extinct viper from the Saharan south. If Johnny recalled well, and if all this was happening and the characters from his book had come to life, the snake wasn't poisonous. That is how Drago, the antique smuggler from the Far East, prevented the people he had kidnapped from counting time and turns so they wouldn't have a clue where they were going. They would quiver and pray the snake doesn't kill them while Drago's man would drive in circles and take the victim to the boss's house. Or a club.

But "what if"s never gave him peace. What if all those people were a bunch of lunatics and what if the snake had venom? Johnny wanted to die. But venom makes you suffer before death, burning and choking on your own chemicals. He hoped it wouldn't last long. His heart was pounding in his chest. And his breath was fast, as if it was in a race with his heartbeats. Who will win, the blood or the air?

He felt like bursting into laughter. The car bumped a few times. The snake crawled over Johnny's head. He tightened the jacket around his neck so the snake couldn't crawl inside, but it was too late. The viper was already in. And it wasn't only in his jacket. It had slipped into his sweater as well. And it wasn't intending to stop.

He started screaming, his body twitching and wriggling, his head hitting the top of the trunk. When the first particle of rationality blinked inside his brain, he pushed at the top of the trunk with both his arms and knees in an attempt to squash the snake. But the trunk was soft for a reason. It was enwrapped by sponges to prevent someone from squashing the snake.

The viper was heading towards the red zone and there was nothing Johnny could do about it. His belt was a one hole looser. The snake slipped under his waistline, crawling between the denim and his cotton boxers that were a little wider around the thighs. This was unfortunate for Johnny, who was shrieking and smashing the trunk with every part of his body. Yet, even he could not hit himself unconscious because the sponge was just too thick. He had to suffer.

Ratio snagged his consciousness for a moment and he remembered how his deceased father used to say that our souls lived in our thoughts. Laughter overpowered him and his cries intertwined with the chortles. He squeezed his butt cheeks but regretted it because it left the snake with no other choice but to proceed to the zone of his progeny.

And then there was the viper, black, thick, and soft, snuggling in between his dick and balls. Johnny was on the brink of puking. His chest and stomach were going numb. He felt the little split tongue darting up and down over his shaft.

A light appeared, the faces floating above dark and blurry. Like a raging bull, Johnny jumped out of the trunk and fell to the concrete. He screamed as he groped for the button on his jeans. The writer wiggled like a madman shoved into a straightjacket for the first time. Most guys believe that they can free themselves but once it gets hold of you, madness never lets you go.

With spit covering his chin, he squinted from the lights blinding him. It felt as if his belt was hiding the prong on purpose. Johnny couldn't form a single word. He tried to wriggle out of his jeans with the belt on, but one hole loose was not enough for a man to slide out: only for a snake to crawl in. He groped at the prong but only kept scratching at the leather strap. He was out of breath. Puke started to form in his mouth.

Then he felt a hand sliding between his palms. His belt was unbuttoned. Johnny tried sliding out of his jeans and boxers, but his shoes were too big and the pieces of clothing couldn't roll over them. With his jeans and underwear around his ankles, Johnny pushed himself backward, using his elbows and legs, the concrete scraping his soft white butt. Unfortunately, his boxers turned into a net that caught the snake along the way. The serpent was hissing and rushing forward. Johnny hit the wall with his back. There was nowhere else to go. Again, the gentle hand appeared and the snake coiled around it.

"Men... If they don't have reason to fight, just throw a snake at their genitals," a woman remarked.

The writer sighed with relief. When his eyes adjusted to the light, he noticed it was not just any woman. It was Indra herself. Panting, with puke and spit trickling down his chin, he mumbled, "Indra? Is that you?"

"Would you be alive if it wasn't?" she inquired, looking at him from above. Her mischievous black eyes shone like jewels.

"This can't be happening. No. It's all in my head... Calm down, Johnny. Calm down."

"Clean him! We have little time," Indra said. "Dominic is losing control."

Only then did Johnny acknowledge that he was lying in a dead-end between two abandoned buildings. The green iron door on the left led one floor underground, where life in Babylon was just starting.

Indra's two companions, more bulldozers than men, ripped his clothes and left him naked on the concrete. Around ten yards away, a yellow fire hydrant was standing on the sidewalk. The bigger guy, named Gentle Ron, approached it, while the other one pulled Johnny to his feet and dragged him to the hydrant.

"What the hell are you gonna do to me?" he mumbled, trying to break free. But the grip was too strong. It felt like he had chains over his chest and a buffalo was pushing him from behind.

Gentle Ron took hold of the fat metal valve and started turning it. It creaked before cracking letting the water spray. The icy stream hit naked Johnny.

The writer was screaming, "Fuck! Cold! Fuck! Fuck! Cold! Stop! Stop! Stop!"

A homeless guy passing stopped to watch.

"That would be enough," said Indra. "It's time to get dressed."

Gentle Ron turned the valve and the water stopped. Johnny was trembling. The brute pulled him back to the Bentley, opened the back door, and pushed him inside. Indra helped him put on a new suit. She assured him he would have a delightful time shortly.

The writer was still in shock, but when he got out of the car, all squared up in his black suit with a blue tie falling over his pink shirt, he felt that he could think rationally. And he even felt good after glimpsing his reflection in the Bentley's window.

As they approached a door in one of the buildings, it opened. A slow-faced kiddo covered with rose petals rushed out. A big-nosed midget darted after him, shouting that he was in big trouble. A big guy in a coat emerged, leaving the door open. Johnny had no idea who they were, nor did he have time to think about it. Indra rushed through the door, down the narrow stairs, and through a long, dark corridor.

At the end, a tall black man with enormous arms was standing in front of a round iron door with a wheel. It looked more like the entrance of a safe than a club. As the four of them approached, Johnny recognized the doorman. It was Jeremiah. He was a mercenary from Africa who had fought in World War Two all over North Africa and had later traveled to Argentina to chase Nazis. When he caught and killed the ones he held responsible for the death of his family, Jeremiah had come north to the promised land—the U.S. He hadn't had a single penny in his pocket.

This being some time ago, no one had wanted to employ him because of his skin color and thick foreign tongue. So he had boxed on the docks to buy himself food. Light on his legs, with heavy fast arms, he had knocked down all of his opponents during the first round and soon made it to the professional ring. Experts predicted him a hell of a career. However fighting was not enough to make a decent living: it all went to the promoters and the gamblers. At least not before the first title fight. Instead, Jeremiah had accepted jobs in nightclubs and had found work as a bouncer. One night he beat a short fat guy who slapped a stripper. It turned out the guy was a rich Jew who owned half of the coast and held a few judges in his pocket. Jeremiah got two years in prison and permanently lost his boxing license. When he got out, all he could do was bounce. And there he was, standing in front of Babylon.

Jeremiah made a step forward and said, "Unless this here is God himself, he cannot enter if he isn't on the list. And I am here long enough to know all the faces on the list."

"This is God," Indra replied. "In a way."

"I doubt it," Jeremiah said disdainfully.

"We are all gathered here because of him. You must let him in," Indra urged.

"It's not my job to know why people gather," he replied. "My job is only to make sure no one who isn't on the list gets in. So, unless he is God, he will not enter."

"Easy, guys," Indra said and pulled Gentle Ron and her other big man back. "We don't want any trouble."

"Trouble? With these clowns?" Jeremiah chuckled conceitedly. "I could fight them with only my left hand while scratching my ass with the right."

"You watched from the closet while your sister was conceived. Your mother fought bravely, but the burglars were just too strong and too many. You froze while your panties turned wet and warm. You were only five years old but have never forgiven yourself. And have never told anyone… Not even your sister," Johnny recalled.

Jeremiah swallowed hard. "I don't know what you are talking about," he said, trying to sound tough, but his voice quivered.

"You swore never to be weak again. That is why you started training. Carrying stones. Waging wars. Chasing

Nazis to avenge your mother and sister. And beating the Jew," Johnny looked at him significantly. "Yes… I know. Your mother danced to survive. You saw her when you were seven. Amber was barely two years old, and she needed milk and diapers. You didn't believe your friends when they told you. You sneaked into the house of pleasure and saw her on the pole. And when here, the Jew slapped that stripper, you knew who he was. But you wanted him to suffer, nevertheless."

Jeremiah couldn't utter a word. He turned, jerked at the wheel, and pulled the door open. Johnny, Indra, Gentle Ron, and the fourth guy entered.

3

The saxophones shone like gold. The old Jazz melody dating from between the two world wars vibrated through the warm, smoke-filled air. Seven musicians, black as night, in red suits, aligned by height, clustered into a crescent on the stage. They were rocking in their chairs as they tapped the keys and puffed their cheeks, the saxophones swaying like babies in their mothers' arms. The musicians' shadows grew to ten feet high on the velvet red curtains behind them. Five girls in short fluttery dresses, high heels, and translucent pantyhose glided between the musicians, throwing their legs up and down to the rhythm.

All the round tables were occupied. The guests' voices merging with the music. Faces were enveloped in smoke and the shadows seemed familiar. At the table next to the corner of the stage, a fat Nazi general with a swastika around his upper arm raised a black girl's ankle. She was smiling, her foot high above his face. He removed her shoe, kissed her sole in white nylon, and set her foot at the table's edge.

Then he took the champagne bottle, filled her shoe, lifted it, and cheered with his companions. Bottoms up followed. Champagne spilled down his chin as he put the shoe tip in his mouth and raised it.

His name was Johan. He was the Desert Fox's right hand and had earned his fortune by smuggling pilfered antiques. When his side started losing the war, he helped Jews escape from the camps, which brought him even more money. When the war was over, Johan fled to Argentina and lived there happily ever after. Their gazes met, and the German winked at Johnny before returning his gaze to the African foot he was worshipping.

Sliding between tables towards the empty place in between, Johnny recognized George from the "Kingdom of Heaven." He was having dinner with his second wife, Eve. George was a warden in the asylum and had urges to eat his wives to ensure they forever remained a part of him. He had killed and eaten his first spouse, Lilith, and was preparing to do the same with the second. However, George loved Eve too much and could not lie to her. So he admitted it to her. Eve was shocked at first but accepted under one condition: Since she was dying from cancer, he had to call her sister and parents to dinner after the funeral and feed them with her infested body parts. He agreed.

Johnny spotted old Richard from "We Need no Reasons." Richard lived a family life with his beautiful Marta, whom he had married immediately after high school. They had grown kids and grandsons who visited them on holidays.

There would be nothing special about Richard if it wasn't for his secret hobby. He was killing cats and burying them in his yard. The yard was full of strange flowers that he never planted, and his garden won prizes in the gardening competitions.

Beautiful Kayla from the "Infinite Pleasure" was there too. She was a bisexual prostitute with the prettiest feet Johnny had ever imagined. Her story was about a client who promised her millions if she endured nine nights of Dante's Inferno. She was sitting with her lady friends, drinking Campari and gossiping. Briefly, Kayla smiled at Johnny.

Indra, Gentle Ron, Rough Oliver - the writer remembered the other guy's name, and Johnny took their seats at a table near the center. Johnny still wasn't sure that all of this was actually happening. Yet, there was a ghost of a smile on his lips, the melody flying out from the golden saxophones lifting him.

"You are better already," Indra noticed.

"What are we doing here?" Johnny asked.

"Negotiating. All these people want you to live," she replied. "We decided to make a party in your honor. This is your night."

"My night. Or the night of death of common sense," Johnny replied.

Gentle Ron was sipping champagne while the server brought plates of sushi and caviar.

"Do you feel it?" Indra asked.

"Feel what?"

"The air? It's like inhaling hope. Or something," she answered.

"The air in Babylon was also filled with promise. Just like every place built after the Great War. In them, breathing meant inhaling hope, since only after so many deaths did people come to enjoy life's simple privileges," Gentle Ron said.

Johnny smiled listening to the quote from his book. Indra looked at him as she sipped her white wine.

"Inhaling hope. It does feel like that," Johnny muttered. "Yet hope is hell's most important ingredient."

"And hell ends once we accept who we are," Indra said.

"Or forget," Johnny added.

"Johnny… Good, old Johnny," Indra chirped. "With your reincarnations, you have taught me that the new things we get are the old things we forget. And we can't completely forget anything."

"I am thinking that this is all in my head."

"Would that make it any less real?" Indra asked.

"No… I…"

"Listen," Oliver interrupted him. "Indra can be too subtle. I like to play with open cards. We don't give a fuckwad about what you think, or how you feel. We want to live. And for us to live, you must live too. At least until all your future books are published. When we get to the bookstores, we will be good even if you do go and kill yourself. That would make you even more popular. There is no greater sensation than a writer who shot his brains out."

"Or jumped into a river and disappeared under mysterious circumstances," Ron added.

"We are born when we are created. And we live when we are read," Indra said. "Your books in the bookstores would mean eternal lives for all of us."

Johnny laughed. He pulled himself together and asked, "Could you call me the warden?"

Indra turned around, raised a hand and motioned to the warden to join them. He stood and arrived with Eve.

"I am honored," he said shaking hands with the writer. Eve smiled and curtsied before sitting.

"Go on… Ask him whatever you wish," Indra prompted Johnny.

"Is this some defense mechanism my mind is playing on me so I will feel important and choose not to kill myself?" Johnny asked.

"Ask Dominic that question and see what happens when he rips your heart out," George replied.

Johnny laughed, turning the glass of whiskey between his fingers. "You are nuts, just like everyone in that madhouse you work in."

"All right. Let's say you have imagined all this. Let's say that when your gun backfired, you suffered a tremendous shock that caused brain trauma and that is making you live this hallucinations. So what? Are hallucinations less real than the rest of what we perceive?" the warden asked pointedly.

"What are we doing here then? I thought…"

"Listen," the warden interrupted. "We are here to persuade you to keep fighting for what you deserve. And we will do everything in our power to provide you with such joy that the mere memory of this night will be enough for you to wish to keep living so you can keep experiencing the memory of it – living and fighting to get us into the bookstores."

Johnny sighed, "Listen... Life is hard enough. We have to wipe our asses while waiting to die. Let alone if you are a broke hedonist in love with beauty. I tried to make my way for decades. But I never hooked a bigger publisher. Let alone hit the bestseller list. It's not meant to be. I feel as if some greater force isn't letting me seize what I believe that I deserve."

Everyone burst out laughing.

"What can we say?" the warden asked, panting. "You wrote me so that I eat every woman I fall in love with so she can become part of me and turn my soul into your kingdom of heaven."

"And I," Eve piped in. "I am a woman dying of cancer who likes the idea that my corrupted body parts will be served to my family. How sick do you have to be?"

"Do you think we like to beat people to death all the time?" Gentle Ron asked. "Of course not. I mean, when I strangled Lewis, the last victim, I didn't even feel I was the one controlling my arms. And the day before, you made me kick his head. And the day before that, I had to snap his neck... God..."

"Ah, yes… changing ugly chapters! The worst thing ever," Oliver agreed.

"What do you think the best death would be?" Johnny asked.

"I think there could be a day in my life without death for a change," Ron replied.

"I don't want to cut people into pieces anymore," Oliver said.

Only Indra was silent. She was looking down, her eyes filled with a wiggling layer of moisture, as if tears were going to spill out at any moment.

When Johnny opened his mouth to address her, a sudden clash pulled his gaze towards the stage. The dancers and musicians were gone and the entire stage had sunken into the shadow except for one circle of light. A short-haired blonde lady, white as snow, stood in the middle, her silver dress covered in shiny diamonds, fluttering around her thighs as she moved her legs slightly, balancing in high glass heels. She parted her red lips and sirens carried her words into the air.

There is a place for us…
There is a place for us in heaven,
There is a place for us in hell
There is a place for us…
We are the children of the seven,
We are born in the sun of heaven,
We are the light of stars,
Night Heaven is full of scars…

Her voice pierced Johnny's body and almost lifted him from the chair. Madelyn was her name. She was from the "Song For the Grave" novel that one of the best publishing houses in New York almost published. But there had always been something standing between Johnny and success. When Johnny returned his gaze to Indra, she looked better. Her dim face with its big beautiful lips smiled.

"Am I pretty?" Indra asked, looking him straight in the eye.

"Just as I imagined," he replied.

"Her beauty was magical. For those who looked at her face, it was never the same. There was always a new wonder to admire. Her eyes never changed. They are the mirrors of infinity," she said.

The writer smiled sadly. "It's beautiful to hear part of one's book. Sad to know that the words only come out of the mouths of your characters."

"Do you want me?"

Johnny was surprised. He was both confused and astonished.

"You can have any woman in this room. Or all of us." The never-ending depths in her gaze pierced him. "Do you want me?"

"Aren't you with Dominic?"

"Yes," she giggled.

"Shouldn't you love him?"

"I do. With every heartbeat. And I will do everything to save him. And you," she said.

"You can have me," Eve chimed in. "I am a good fuck, right?" She asked her husband.

"You are, my darling," the warden replied. "Yes, you are…"

"So…? Who shall it be? Or should we orgy? Do you want the ladies to fight for you? If I remember right, the loser gets fucked?" Indra said.

"But that is from The Hedonist. How do you know about that?" Johnny asked.

"In one way or another, you mention this club in all your books. And when we all started gathering here to chat, your cute little Sarah told us everything," Indra said.

Johnny went to answer, but a loud murmuring overpowered the music. It felt to him as if ants were crawling into his ears and under his skin. Fear crept on the faces that were around, their gazes buzzing like a fly trapped in a jar. Shadows passed over the lights on the stage, painting it red. The air smelled like death. They could no longer inhale hope now that the presence of agony chased it away. Johnny stared at Indra. Her face was frightened as well. Ron, Oliver, George, and Eve stood no better.

Then, just as suddenly, it passed. Madelyn stood still for a few moments before she resumed singing.

If you're happy and you know it, clap your hands
If you're happy and you know it, clap your hands
If you're happy and you know it and you really want to show it
If you're happy and you know it, clap your hands…

"Dominic is here," Indra said, getting up. "He cannot restrain himself any longer. He barely pulled himself away when we put you in the trunk. He will kill us all. I must go. Johnny… I told you. This is your night. Let your imagination gift you whatever you want." Ron and Oliver left with Indra.

"If you will excuse us, my wife and I have to discuss a thing or two about cooking," the warden said, chuckling. They shook hands. Johnny remained alone.

He knew it was not Dominic. It was the messenger who appeared in the chapter before the final one. He had come to tell Indra there was still hope. That Dominic had found a loophole. It was only an introduction to the suffering in the last chapter when they realized it was all a lie.

Lighting a big Cohiba, he thought of Indra and her grim fate. After Dominic, she was the second main character in the novel "Never Mind the Sun." It was a story about a powerful immortal vampire, Dominic, cursed to roam the world for eternity. Almost nothing could kill him. Not the Sun, nor the Moon, nor even a thousand bites of golden vipers on the Island of Snakes. Some would consider him blessed rather than doomed. But there was a second part to the curse. And it held the key to his power and immortality.

Every hundred years, he was forced to rip out his soul-mate's heart and eat it. Otherwise, he would die. Death had always been his choice from the very beginning. But he was not the one to decide. Every century, Dominic would encounter the reincarnation of his soul mate. Many times, during many lives, from Babylon to New York, they would meet, fall in love, and Dominic would kill her in the end. The vampire tried to evade their reunions. To starve himself to death. As the end of the century neared he would lose control over his actions and all his magnificent power would focus on only one thing—ripping the heart of the one he loved and eating it again.

Coincidences turned into causes and consequences hell-bent on connecting the two of them by any and all means. When he, in the tenth century, chained himself to the bottom of the ocean beneath the Northern Pole, a whale ate him and spat him out near the shores of Norway. The water then brought him to the beach, where his future bride was waiting for her husband to return from a raid. The waves pushed him on the sand right after Helga found out Bjorn was killed while charging the castle gates of the enemy king. With her eyes full of tears, she took in the stranger to nurture him back to life instead. Dominic was only frozen and recovered in less than two days. People from the village called it the mercy of gods.

Dominic thought of leaving, but feared the scenario from Sparta could repeat. There he rejected her after they had met and kept himself away in the mountains of far Asia. The distance only strengthened his urges and wilders. He could hear her heartbeats and smell her hair from the thousands of miles away. It had taken him less than a day to return to Sparta and seize her as his prey. When he arrived, he was more beast than a man. Before ripping out her heart, he slew her children in her wheat field right in front of her. That was the only time he saw a suffering greater than his. From then on, he decided to do everything he could to stay after they'd meet for the first time to prevent an even bigger tragedy.

The next year they married and shared the bed in a cottage on top of the rocky hill above the sea for half a century. Then, the night Helga was on her deathbed, and he was still young and strong as if he had just turned twenty, he let the curse take over and reduce him to his darkest instincts. Dominic looked her straight in the eyes while he squeezed her neck. He looked at her long enough to see the world inside her collapsing as she gasped, "What are you doing to me, my love?" before ripping out her heart. After devouring it, Dominic went on a lonely pilgrimage over the icy wasteland, wishing for one thing: to disappear. There he cursed whoever was responsible for the torment he was living without even knowing the reason for his damnation. He fantasized about catching the culprit and grinding his bones into dust. Doing it slowly. Holding him in a cell and torturing him over the years. Bringing him to the brink of death and then helping him recover so he could do it all over again. More than anything, he wanted to be the one to die. He visited every warlock and witch in the world searching for answers. Nobody knew what could trigger such a curse or how to remove it.

As echoes, Dominic heard and saw glimpses of memories from his previous lives. They took place in other worlds where he too had to slay his own children. Those drafts were the versions that Johnny discarded. His editor considered them too brutal. The vampire who could not have children and would fight against his instincts with all his might was a more acceptable solution.

Dominic's soulmate was born a Hindu fortune-teller named Indra. She could recall her previous lives and comprehend the grim fate she and her lover shared. The end of another century was nearing. Dominic's killing instincts were growing stronger. He struggled to avoid Indra at all costs because he would kill her at any moment if she was near. That is why he postponed confronting the writer while she was with him. Although he knew he was going to kill her, Dominic tried to fight his instincts. He provided himself with measured dosages of her presence at different times to avoid turning into a beast. This time he hoped that he would have enough willpower to starve himself to death. But every time, it had ended the same.

While Johnny thought of "Never Mind the Sun" and wondered if this time he could save his protagonist without impairing his masterpiece, his gaze met the big, round eyes of the most beautiful African girl sitting next to Johan. Anaya smiled at him. She stood up and, in her long black dress with a deep side slit, swayed her hips approaching his table.

"Excuse me, are these seats taken?"

"None are taken," he replied.

"I thought loneliness was sitting all around you," she said, taking a seat across from him.

4

In a fluttery purple dress that barely covered the upper half of her thighs, Kayla approached gracefully in her black open-toe heels. She too sat down, turning her naked back to Anaya. She ran her fingers through her long, wavy, sandy hair and smiled.

"I am honored to meet you," she said, putting one of her feet onto the writer's lap.

"You should be honored to be so beautiful," the writer replied as he took hold of Kayla's foot. He removed her shoe, slipped his hand under her ankle, lifted her foot to his face, and kissed it. His lips sank into skin as soft as a feather pillow in a silk pillowcase.

"Honored by you?" she asked. "That is why I came to this table. On a night as special as this, you deserve more than any monkey."

The writer reached for Kayla's other shoe off, looking into her shining eyes. Suddenly, her expression filled with shock. Anaya's hands were deep in her hair. Kayla's face grimaced. As her body was turned upside down, her mouth opened wide, but nary a sound came out. Kayla's legs ran through the air, her feet convulsing wildly. Together with the tablecloth, plates, food and drink, she fell to the floor.

Her body shook like a leaf on the wind as she gripped Anaya's wrists, trying to remove them from her hair. But the woman from Africa was just too strong. A big black foot landed on Kayla's stomach. Kayla moaned, her face crumpling in pain, she couldn't breathe. Her hands fell on her belly as she struggled to push the foot to the side. Anaya's leg was firm like a pillar. A jewel in the trash, the writer thought, looking at Kayla lying there and wriggling in the crumpled tablecloth, fighting for another breath.

Anaya pulled at her. Kayla's body flew like a feather. Creams and sauces smeared her gentle skin. With her legs bent and spread wide, she glided over the floor in between the tables. A few groans escaped her mouth. It looked like she was trying to say, "Let me go," but was too shocked for words. Anaya pulled her under the stage and climbed up. As she was approaching the stairs, Kayla managed to stand up and punch her opponent. Yet that punch was like a mosquito bashing into the wall during its flight. Anaya didn't feel a thing. So she plunged one hand into Kayla's hair and shook her. The girl was barely keeping her ground. Anaya played with her as if Kayla was a rag doll which she had decided to rip apart. She was slapping her, throwing her on the floor, and pulling her up. Kayla's moans merged with the sounds of slaps as she waved her hands in front of her face to defend herself. The guests cheered and laughed.

Johnny came to the stage, a spike jutting from his pants. He felt as if he was going to split his progeny at any moment. Anaya threw Kayla on her back and mounted her. Kayla's legs were bent and spread. She tried to push herself back but her soles, wet and slippery from the sauces and creams, slid over the shiny stage, leaving a messy trail behind. Her shaved clam resembled a smooth one-eyed crack and stared out at everyone. Anaya trapped Kayla's arms between her thighs. Her soft face was at the mercy of one of her so-called "monkeys". Anaya gathered spit in her mouth.

She let it go slowly. A fat thread of saliva slid from her mouth, hanging over Kayla's face. In vain, she tried to roll and turn her head to the side. Anaya grabbed her jaw with her palms and held it straight. The saliva fell on her cheek, nose and down part of the mouth, ending on the bottom of her chin.

"Let me go!" Kayla squealed.

Her voice was quivering. She was trying to look tough, but fear was spilling from her eyes. Anaya said nothing. She spat on her again. This time saliva splashed all over her face. After that, Anaya treated her with a rain of slaps. She mercilessly raised her palms and dropped them right on her cheeks. One hand after another, Kayla's head swung left and right. After a clap, she would release a painful moan. Kayla's face was red and the tears leaking from her eyes had merged with the saliva.

"Beg me to stop!" Anaya boomed.

Kayla resisted. It did not take long for her muffled groans to turn into shrieks. Kayla begged.

"Stop! I beg of you!"

Anaya ignored her. She kept bringing down her palms onto Kayla's face until the poor girl fainted. Even then, Anaya did not intend to stop. After Kayla passed out, her feet slid over the floor until her legs straightened. Her stained bare soles glimmering under the stage lights faced the crowd.

Johnny felt as if his whole body had turned into an erect cock. Kayla's cunt was glimpsing between her thighs. Anaya was ruthlessly slapping her. The sounds of the claps echoed throughout the club. When Anaya's hand landed on her face, Kayla's soles twitched. Occasionally, Anaya would gather saliva and spit on the poor girl's face.

The writer had never seen anything so beautiful. Yet a quiet voice inside his head murmured that it was all wrong. "This might not be real," Johnny repeated to himself as he walked around the stage to see the humiliating show from different angles. Also, it could be, the voice murmured.

Anaya turned towards the crowd and shouted, "Do you think that this bitch has had enough?!"

Silence followed.

"Hell, no!" someone shouted.

"Bash her face into a bloody pulp!"

"Fist her!" another voice sounded before the crowd joined the choir, "Fist! Fist! Fist!"

Johnny jumped in and pulled Anaya back. He gently took Kayla into his arms and went behind the stage. There were a few narrow corridors, and he took the first one. It led him to the club's private suite with a Jacuzzi and a big bed.

He lay Kayla on the red silky sheets and sat beside her. She was breathing slowly, her hair sprawled out on the pillow like a sunflower's petals. Under the muffled lights, the saliva on her face glimmered like morning dew.

She was slow waking up. While bending her knee, her foot sliding over the silk, the fluttery dress fell back revealing her beautiful fruit. There was a blotch of whipped cream on the side of Kayla's cunt. Johnny wanted nothing more than to lick it away. Then dive his tongue deep inside her and inhale the taste of her essence.

"You can lick it if you wish," she said in a tired voice, catching his yearning gaze.

She slowly opened her eyes.

"Are you all right?" he asked.

"I am fine. It's not the first time I got the shit beaten out of me for the joy of men. You should know that best," she said.

"I am sorry. I should have stopped it," he replied.

"Don't worry about it," she said, looking at him straight. "Will you lick me?"

"I will, but first I must…"

She raised her foot and shoved it into Johnny's face.

"I didn't think I would inspire you for a conversation in a state like this," she said.

Johnny stuck out his tongue and gathered the cream from her heel and sole while her foot was gently sliding down. Kayla pushed her toes into his mouth. He started sucking them, his tongue sliding between her toes.

"It feels nice," Kayla said.

She pulled her foot from his head and put it on his groin.

"Would you look at that? The other one is sticky too," she said, lifting her other foot above the writer's face and planting the heel into his open mouth. She pointed the toes to make the sole strained and smooth for Johnny's tongue.

After sliding down his face, she shoved her toes with her nails painted black into his mouth. This time with more force. Johnny swallowed them and used his hands to push the heel forward. He felt his saliva gathering as his tongue slid over the ball of her foot and under the toes that were tickling his throat. He pulled her foot out of his mouth and a thin white thread hung between his lips and her big toe. It broke and fell over her sole.

"I think you should undress," she said.

The writer shed his suit. Kayla lifted her legs in a split, her knees bent loosely. The writer squeezed his balls a few times to prevent himself from coming right away. Then he pierced her. Kayla's cunt was deep and wet like a cave. Johnny slowly moved his hips back and forth, Kayla's feet dangling in the air. Johnny spread his hands out to reach them. She was flexible like gum.

He lay Kayla over, bent her legs, and pulled her feet around their heads. Her groin was wet and warm, her moans vibrating through his skin and bones, their faces almost touching. Kayla turned her head aside and took one foot with both hands. Then she pulled it next to her face and began licking it. Johnny joined her, their tongues meeting on Kayla's sole. As their lips merged, Johnny closed his eyes, their tongues wrestling in the wet darkness like madmen trying to strangle each other. Her kiss was addictive. It tasted of strawberries. He had written her to always chew a gum before pleasing her clients.

When their lips parted, Johnny ran his tongue over her face. He licked and sucked at all of Anaya's liquids. Then he gathered saliva in his mouth, spat, and smeared it all over Kayla's face. Kayla grabbed her other foot and brought it between their mouths. Between their kisses, she spat on her sole and Johnny licked it up.

He came inside her while sucking at her heel. It felt as if all of his progeny had melted into a liquid and filled Kayla's pussy to overflowing. He pulled out his dick and turned to the side. Kayla slid out from her dress and dropped it next to the bed, the writer's sperm trickling from her pussy. She put her fingers into the stream. Kayla put the gathered sperm into her mouth.

"Your sperm is salty. It tastes like seawater," she said.

Both of them chuckled as Kayla mounted him.

"So…," she made a brief pause. "What's up?"

"Nothing," Johnny said.

"I won't lecture you about not killing yourself," she said. "I would like to keep existing because the prize I get after going through the inferno is a rich life until death. I can only imagine how hard it must be for you. You are a man born for pleasure but can't escape poverty. It is the definition of hell."

"Sadly, only a few people get it," Johnny replied. "I had enough of everything."

"I understand. It does make you one interesting guy," she remarked with a smile on her face. "I often go to Babylon and hang with some of my colleagues from 'Stories from the Brothel.' They tell me about you. I met Lara too… Her story was interesting. What she had to say about you could be turned into a big fat book within a book."

Johnny smiled, "A novel within a novel."

"She must be the one," Kayla remarked with a warm look in her eyes.

"To be honest, Lara was ever the only one. The rest of the girls are prostitutes," Johnny said.

"I know. They understand and support you completely," Kayla said. "You are handsome. But the kind of women you like…, you need money. I mean, pedicure, manicure, hairdresser, skin lotions, high heels, dresses, makeup, vacations, dinners, suites money… Their beauty needs nurturing. And nurturing needs cash. A man like you has to find a way to make money. Not in my craziest dreams would I consider proposing that you go out and fuck a broodmare. Settle for a fat ugly cunt who has never heard of pedicures, hairdressers, body lotions or high heels…"

"It is such a relief to hear those thoughts," Johnny said. "I mean…"

"Don't tell me what you mean," Kayla interrupted. "We both share the same pain in our chests from yearning for beauty outside our reach. When I got the offer to go inside the inferno and get millions if I endured, I said to myself, 'Kayla, you are going to have to dive into sewers to escape mediocre.' That is what I did. Let me tell you, if I didn't succeed, I would kill myself rather than set my divine feet inside any public transportation."

"Exactly," Johnny said passionately. "That's my girl."

"You don't mind me being a whore?" Kayla inquired, a mischievous smile on her face.

"What kind of question is that?" Johnny asked in surprise. "You, of all people, know the answer…"

"I do. But every chapter with fucking requires a chit-chat with deep, emotional, wise, or at least funny quotes that you can use to promote your book on social media. And you are, by all means, going to write about the fuck that we just had," she said and both of them chuckled.

"I am. But the conversations should seem natural. They cannot be forced," he said.

"But when a beautiful woman compels you to do something, she does not force it. She inspires it… Let's start over. Do you mind a woman having been a whore?"

"Whore is just one letter away from whole," Johnny said.

Kayla smiled. "I love that guy. He's from the 'Illiterate Psychopath?' Right?"

"Yes, he is," Johnny said.

"I met him in Babylon a few times. We talked. He spoke of religions. How the world came from word. One letter more or less to increase or remove the stress. Push 'A' in front of void. Strip 'K' from what you know to get the only thing you have—now. And his golden rule of life: Spell to avoid hell," she said, chuckling. "Whore, whole. Wife, life. Pick, kick."

"It's hard to turn spelling into a spell when you know how to read," Johnny said. "I think one must be illiterate if one want to remain happy."

"In the inferno, an ugly nun beat and humiliated me. Why did you write that? Do you like to watch pretty girls beaten and humiliated by the ugly ones?" she asked.

"I like to watch beauty struggle. The ugly nun was beating you out of jealousy. And even under her fat ass, dirty, bloody, and in tears, you were all the more beautiful than all the genetic waste in the generations of her family."

"Which reminds me, I have to ask you something." She made a brief pause, looking him in the eye. "Did I squeal too much when Anaya was beating me on the stage?"

"Yes… You were perfect," Johnny said.

When their eyes reconnected, his dick hardened straight toward her pussy.

"You like to watch beauty struggle, eh?" she moaned.

The writer remained silent. He was as hard as a stone.

"Do you know why the nun beat the crap out of me?" she asked.

"I told you," the writer replied. "Jealousy. It had nothing to do with you tempting the monks into debauchery. To her, God and religion were just an excuse."

"You forget," she said, moving forward just enough for her groin to brush his cock and make it choke on his progeny.

"Forget what?"

"That you were drunk when you wrote and threw those chapters away," she said. "The original chapters were darker.

It was the sixth circle of hell. I was supposed to force the pure-hearted and forgiving nun to become violent. I had to enrage the nun and return her unconditional love and kindness with the worst behavior."

Johnny's face melted into a grim smile. "What did you do?"

"When I arrived at the monastery, the nun, Gabriella, gave me food and shelter. She accepted me as a daughter and fed me and even did my portion of work, since everyone in the monastery must work. After two weeks, your client sent me a message that it was time to start. First, I fucked all the priests and monks in the monastery and made them fight over me. Then I went to the village where Gabriella's two sisters lived with their husbands. The husbands were brothers, the two families having known each other for generations before they merged through marriage. Their properties bordered. I fucked them both. One by one. They threw out their wives, her sisters, because of me. Wives and kids, both. Divorced in a matter of weeks. I married the older brother in the monastery right in front of Gabriella. But she was hard to tempt to rage. That fat old cow blessed us instead. She kissed me and told me she wasn't angry and that God has mysterious ways," Kayla told him. "But then, as soon as we got married, I fucked with his brother and had them fight over me all over again. My new husband was both wiser and stronger. But the younger brother would not stand to be defeated. He was too vain to lose. He took his gun and wounded his brother. Then he fucked me victoriously. I brought him to the monastery.

There, I fucked him deep into the night. When he filled my cunt with his sperm, I held it tight, sneaked to Gabriella's room, climbed…"

"Climbed onto her bed. I remember," Johnny interrupted.

"Let me say it," Kayla said. "I climbed onto her bed, spread my legs above her face, and let the sperm flow right into her mouth."

"The devil's whore," Johnny said.

"When she asked me what I was doing, I told her everything. Hearing that her sisters' ex-husbands had almost killed each other, made her go insane. She pulled me by my hair and dragged me through the halls of the monastery. As she pulled me, she bashed my head with her fat fist. I flew through the corridors, screaming for my life. I thought I would need surgery after she was done with my face. I remember my feet sliding over a trail of piss that was leaking out of me. It was mostly the wine that I had drank that night.

All the monks and priests that I had fucked watched as she taught me their basic decency. When she tired of smashing my head into the corridor walls, she dragged me out of the monastery and ripped at my clothes. She held me by the hair and paraded me in front of all the monks who gathered to watch. They were jerking below their robes. I was naked and afraid, my face a bloody pulp.

Under all that pain, something pleasant sprouted in my womb. Gabriella screamed that I was the devil's whore! She dropped me in the mud, kneeled onto my chest with all her weight, and bashed her fists all over my face. She was heavy. I was losing my breath and couldn't feel my body, leaking from all my holes. Piss, shit, blood, and spit, I suppose.

Suddenly, my cunt began contracting." While she was speaking and gently swaying on his groin, Johnny's dick began to twitch. "I just started splashing. I never felt more joy in my life. Gabriella jumped away from me. She had no idea what was going on. My entire body was convulsing. And all the priests and monks gathered and poured their liquid seed all over me."

Johnny was groaning. He felt like every atom of his body had grown a cock and was coming. The pleasure was so strong that he almost fainted.

"I am a slut! I live to drive men insane. And get beaten by their wives," Kayla concluded. "I was written that way."

"Evil and beautiful," he said.

"I don't think it's evil," she retorted. "I do what must be done to seize what I want. This sometimes makes me wonder, do fighters ever get prizes? Or only consolations for who they were before burying themselves to make space for that new person capable of doing what needs to be done? Because if someone told me I was going to fuck up two brothers the way I did, before I accepted the inferno game, I would have told them that they are insane."

"I know what you mean. But tell me, what was the hardest assignment of all?" Johnny inquired.

"The ninth circle, diving into the sea of sperm," Kayla said.

"Forgive the intrusion." Indra barked as she barged into the room. "We have to leave right away."

Her eyes were shining and her face barely refrained from melting into a smile.

"What happened?" the writer asked.

"Dominic found the loophole," Indra said.

Johnny smiled, looking at her sadly.

"I will stay."

"Either you get your ass up by yourself or Oliver and Ron will do it for you. It's completely up to you," Indra snapped.

"There is no loophole," Johnny said.

"There is. He sent his messenger to tell me. He found the ancient necklace. If carried…"

"You can break any curse on the night of the alignment of seven far stars. Let me guess, tonight is the night?"

Indra frowned.

"It is the final chapter. The one when the two of you realize there is no salvation," he said.

"You are wrong," Indra replied.

"Am I?"

"Tonight, you will learn about life. And realize that life is unpredictable. And most important of all, you will learn that, with faith, everything is possible," Indra said with determination. "Now, either get the fuck up and come with me or I will call Oliver and Ron to help you. It's your choice."

5

Johnny got up from the bed and dressed. As he passed through the club, the music stopped. Madelyn bowed and said, "Ladies and gentlemen, let's applaud the man responsible for all of us being here tonight."

The guests stood up and applauded. Johnny smiled, raised his arms, and waved. The applause invigorated him. He bowed and sent a kiss before going out the door.

"These people want nothing more but to keep existing," Indra said as they walked down the corridor.

"They are crazy... but so is their writer," Johnny retorted.

They chuckled, climbed the stairs, and went out of the building.

When they reached the car, a thin voice called from behind, "Hey, mister. Do you have a penny to spare?"

They turned and saw a little boy in brown pants with suspenders and a gray hat. He was holding a colt. His entire body was shaking. The boy was aiming for Johnny, but the barrel was wavering over all of them. He got a hold of himself.

As his finger pulled the trigger, Oliver rushed in front of the writer. His chest took the bullet. The giant swayed a few steps forward before crashing onto the concrete. The boy threw the gun and ran.

"Oh, my God!" Gentle Ron cried out and fell to his knees. "My beautiful Oliver!"

Oliver was hyperventilating. The little red blur on his white shirt was quickly widening. In a few moments, it spread under the lapels of his elegant jacket. He raised his hand, and Ron squeezed it.

"Can you tell?" Oliver whispered.

"No, no you can't!" Gentle Ron wept. "You will be fine!" He lowered his head and kissed Oliver's palm while his other arm gently caressed his cheek. "You will be fine! Will someone call the fucking ambulance?"

"Don't cry," Oliver mumbled and turned his gaze to Johnny, his glassy eyes looking at the writer like he was a shrine. He asked, "Could my Jenny go to Harvard? She can multiply four-digit numbers in her head."

His lips became motionless, his eyes wide open, looking at Johnny. It looked like he was still alive, but his chest wasn't moving anymore. Ron wept. Indra leaned her head onto his big shoulder.

"We have to go," she whispered. "They are coming."

"Who is coming?" Johnny asked, his heart beating fast. He wondered if suicide was what he really wanted.

"Dominic is not the only one who wants to kill you. He is only the most powerful," she said.

A crowd appeared in the mouth of the valley, seven short, thin men in black suits and red ties walking in front, their faces pale as snow and their bald heads smooth as ice on a frozen lake.

"Oh, fuck," Johnny mumbled.

He recognized them right away. The seven pale brothers. All born with leukemia. All raped by their cruel stepfather. All married to wives who died while giving birth to dead-born babies. They were the owners of the big casino and were in charge of the city. The last man who refused to pay them racket watched as they gouged the eyes of his three-year-old son. They walked as if their feet were feathers. Nobody could hear them coming. Followed by the crowd, they approached slowly, their faces on the edge of a smile, their eyes cold and dull with the madness in their depths.

"We must go!" Indra said.

Ron remained kneeling beside Oliver. Johnny tried to pull him up but the guy was as heavy as a truck.

Johnny's main characters started coming out of the nightclub, some of them brandishing baseball bats, golf clubs, and knives. Except Jeremiah. He would be insulted if someone even thought of offering him a weapon besides his fists. They made a wall in front of the writer's little fellowship.

There wasn't a single shout when the groups collided. Only the sounds of stabs and the crunching of bones. The writer saw Jeremiah's fist go right through the youngest pale brother's skull. He fell to the ground where he remained motionless. As the boxer punched his demolishing right hook, one of the pale brothers stepped in and stabbed him between the ribs. The warden bit the stabber's neck. A crazy purple-haired slut jumped the warden from behind and shoved her nails into his face. Jeremiah remained on his feet, but his body spasmed. He could still throw the jab. Johan was under the feet of several black-clad teenagers who were stomping him ruthlessly. He was paying for all the torture they suffered in school from the skinheads.

Kayla and Anaya teamed up against Lea, the hundred-kilo bearded bitch who suffered from an inborn hormone disorder. The bottom of her clit had some strange shit resembling a little cock and she was as strong as a lumberjack. The girls were flying in her arms.

Golf clubs were falling on skulls while blood splashed everywhere. Bodies fell and rarely got back up.

There was not a single gunshot. It was as if they had made a deal to settle their fates the old-fashioned way. And those who wanted the writer to live were losing the battle. As one pale brother broke through the wall, someone broke his head with a golf club. Blood splashed all around him and he fell straight on his face.

Ron got to his feet and hurried to the driver's seat. Johnny and Indra jumped behind. The Bentley crushed through the crowd. He ran over a dying Jeremiah, Eve, two pale brothers, and a few of the gypsy kids armed with stones.

"Oh, my God! You killed them!" the writer shouted as the Bentley rushed through the fighting, the back door remaining open. As the car bounced, Johnny flew back and almost fell out. Indra caught his jacket and pulled him in just seconds before his head touched the concrete.

"Holy fuck!" he yelled as he slammed the door. "Is there a fucking end to this madness?!"

"Who was that kid that shot Oliver? I've never heard of any boy," Indra asked, the car racing down the street, followed by the other angry drivers' curses.

"He is from the New York Gardens," Johnny replied. "His father was a forensic psychiatrist who wanted to see how murdering at a young age affected the psyche. So he showed him names and pictures of random faces, explaining that all the people he kills are hard-core criminals and that he is doing society a favor."

"Oh my God," Indra whispered and shook her head.

"To his younger brother," Johnny resumed, "he promised money for every murder committed without delving into the victims' identities. He wanted to see how murdering with different motivations would influence their psyches."

"I don't understand why you are doing that." Gentle Ron turned his head from the road. "Is this some kind of self-exploration? Traveling through your dark thoughts and writing them down to free yourself from them?! Or are you fucking bored and find other people's torments funny?"

"The road, Ron!" Indra yelled, the car bumping and their bodies hopping inside like popcorn inside a hot pot.

"I don't know what it is and I don't give a fuck why you do it!" Ron went on. "But Jenny goes to Harvard or I will do things to you that will leave you too depressed to even attempt suicide."

"Leave him be," Indra said.

"Guys, I am afraid we have company," Johnny mumbled timidly, looking through the back window.

"Do I want to know?" Indra asked as the black limo with tinted windows approached.

"The rich conjoined twins, Jim and Jack. They fell in love with the same woman. Needless to say, she was a prostitute. They fought for her, and Jack strangled Jim. However, it turned out Jim's brain was in charge of erections, so Jack couldn't fuck her on his own," Johnny explained.

"Why are you so sick?" Ron yelled.

"They are never alone," Johnny added.

Two pickup trucks with mercenaries holding machine guns were following the limo. They easily passed the limousine and opened fire. Bullets pierced the glass but only made cracks. Johnny screamed and fell under the seat, covering his head with his hands. Indra was sitting as if nothing was happening. Ron stepped on the gas and the acceleration threw Johnny's body onto the back of the front seat. The shooting continued. The mercenaries had the newest generation of machine guns, which made explosions when firing bullets that could pierce through ten skulls behind fifty inches of metal. It was a miracle that the windows were still standing.

"Are you fucking insane?" Johnny yelled at Indra. "Get the fuck down."

"I might not know everything, but this is not my time," she replied. "Nor is it Ron's."

The back window burst, and shards of glass fell all over the back seats. Bullets buzzed inside the car next to Indra's and Ron's heads but they behaved like they were sitting and sipping tea.

"Who the fuck is crazy in this car?" Johnny shouted. The front window exploded. Another rain of glass fell. The air streamed like a hurricane.

"Would you please have faith?" Indra asked, looking at him from above. Only then did Johnny notice that his head was under her yellow skirt. Her feet were tucked in black suede pumps, but Johnny knew her toes were gorgeous and probably painted red. "Could you please," she repeated loudly while bullets were roaring and flying around them, "Could you please, for a change, have faith and sit as it fits a mature man?"

"Fucking bullets flying around!"

"I can see the future, and I assure you that nothing will happen to either of us."

"I don't trust your fucking foretelling abilities!"

The car bumped as the front of the limo hit it from behind. The Bentley swerved and its tires squeaked like a wounded duck. Ron almost lost control of the vehicle. Beeping was coming from everywhere. They were speeding down streets and intersections as if they were in their private racing lot. Ron successfully evaded the other drivers, but the limo and pickup trucks were turning upside down every car that crossed their path.

Indra put her hand on Johnny's head. "Take a leap of fate."

"This is a fucking life and death situation!" Johnny shouted.

"Everything is. You did, after all, want to kill yourself, didn't you!?"

Johnny braced himself and climbed on the back seat. He could feel bullets flying around his head. He was panting, and his entire body trembled.

"Let it go!" Indra shouted.

"Let go of what!?"

"Your fears! A man who decides to kill himself is already dead! And what is dead cannot be killed!"

"Don't you GOT me," Johnny yelled. Then he closed his eyes and took a deep breath.

Just after the Bentley passed through an intersection, a transport truck appeared from the side and bashed into the limo and pickup trucks. Johnny turned to see the explosion.

"They are gone," Indra said.

"For someone who wanted to kill himself, you sure worry about your life," Ron noticed, turning into a windy street leading to the highway.

"No one wants to die. People who choose suicide only want their suffering to stop," Johnny snapped.

"Suffering stops when we decide to achieve peace," Indra said. "Did you see what you just did?"

"What?"

"The truck at the intersection. That was your doing," Indra said.

"Come on! Shut the fuck up! That wasn't me!" Johnny protested. But his voice sounded doubtful even to him.

"Hopefully, when this is over, you will learn that we never know what the next morning is going to bring," Indra said before letting the silence envelop them.

...

The writer was sitting with his head leaning on the edge of the window and watching the sky. Dark clouds were everywhere. Strangely, the writer thought of the stars while gazing at them.

He heard a child's laughter coming from above. His face split into a smile. Johnny recalled his father giving him his first book, "The Little Prince." The boy promised the pilot that every star would laugh after his departure and remind him of his friend from the desert who would be somewhere above, with his beloved flower. It wasn't only the laughter. He remembered his father reading him the book so many times. Johnny didn't recall his face while he was alive. He remembered the expression on his corpse. One morning, Johnny's mother got a call from the police station. Her husband had committed suicide. Hung himself in the forest. He was still warm when a man jogging by pulled him down and called an ambulance. Johnny went to see him. His father was pale, pain carved into his frozen face, a thin red line circling his neck.

"Your father was a powerful man. And your mother is a very strong woman… you are strong as well. You should not be hard on yourself. It's difficult to live like everyone else when you are different," Indra whispered and gently took his hand.

"I am not sure about anything anymore," Johnny admitted. "Sometimes it feels like suicide is the only thing a man can truly choose to do. Everything else is a painful enforcement…"

"It's not like that," Indra said. "Life is full of chances and choices."

"But it isn't… Choice is an illusion. Our hearts beat as they please, our lungs breathe when they want… Our legs travel the paths carved long before we were born. All we can do is experience our struggle. Unless we were all divinities who got bored and came to this world to take a rest from the omnipotence, I see no reason why would we choose to keep fighting and grinding when death is inevitable," Johnny said.

"Ol… Oli… My colleague and I liked to hang out with your Little Prince," Ron chimed up. "His soul was pure since he was but a child. He told me that, growing up, he concluded that thinking is a disease. And I just wanted to remind you that you are one sick son of a bitch."

"Ron!" Indra hissed.

"What?"

"Enough! He is not sick! He is a marvel in the world of filth!" Indra blurted out.

Ron turned the wheel and stepped on the brake. Johnny and Indra flew forward and their heads hit against the front seats.

"That guy killed Oliver! He took him from me! He took my mate!" Ron turned and shouted, his face distorted as red as melting lava. "He took my mate! He took… he took my heart!" Ron rushed from the car and strode over the dirt into the dark.

"Give him time… He will be back…" Indra said.

The Bentley was parked next to a highway in the middle of a wasteland. There was nothing except sand and bushes. The only thing that could be heard was the howling of jackals. Occasionally, a roaring engine would sound and a transport truck would rush over the road.

They were silent. In the darkness, Indra was so beautiful, her face gentle and her eyes like jewels no man had ever seen before. She neared Johnny, her lips so close that they almost touched his cheek. He could feel her warm breath on his skin. His groin instantly erected a monument to her beauty. She clutched his jaw and turned his face towards her. Her palm fell over the jutting in Johnny's pants. Their breaths were deep and slow as their gazes quietly collided. She was slowly rubbing his groin while her other hand glided over his cheek. As her lips neared his, Johnny turned to the side. Indra's lips brushed his cheek.

"What's wrong? Don't you want me? I am sure you have a strong desire for me," she remarked, dropping her gaze to his groin.

"It's not that…"

"Seize me," Indra prompted. "Do whatever you wish."

"You are like gravity. Something that I can't comprehend at the moment, and I choose to fly," Johnny said, his voice quivering.

"I am not sure I understand you," Indra said with a bitter smile.

"In a way, you are holy to me," Johnny explained.

Indra burst out laughing and Johnny joined her. He knew she had just read his mind. And a thought had entered that mind: that he should write Indra into a reincarnation who never slept with anyone except Dominic.

"You could desecrate me now and resurrect my innocence later," she suggested.

"I can't. I just can't allow myself to step into something so pure like your love for Dominic," he said.

"You are a true romantic," Indra remarked.

"I am thinking about Oliver setting the world record for time spent in clinical death," Johnny said.

Indra laughed again. "But would such purity and emotion be possible without hardships?"

"I'm afraid not."

6

Thunders were roaring like God was pealing the skin from the sky. Lightning pierced the darkness long enough for the house on the top of the hill to appear.

"I'll be damned," Johnny exclaimed as the Bentley approached. "The trauma must be enormous."

Behind the house and under the hill, a town sprawled. But it wasn't just any town. It was the one from "The Reaper's Hell." Red lights blazed behind windows covered with thin curtains. There were about fifty houses, all of them brothels working twenty-four/seven. Some of the ladies working in them were the ones Jack the Reaper killed during his earthly pilgrimages.

The only man living in the town was Jack the Reaper, the catch being that he could not kill any woman, but they could kill him the same way he killed them. However, he could not see the murder coming, the memories of his wrongdoings erased. He was therefore unable to recognize his victims and expect retaliation. Neither could he remember his death after resurrecting in this, his hell. All the tortures he suffered were to haunt him in his nightmares, the faces of his executioners blurry. The house on the top of the hill was the place the devil visited once a year to see how the great London butcher was doing. Most of the time, it stood empty.

"He is waiting for us," Indra said.

Reaching the low spiky fence, they exited the Bentley, though Ron remained in the car. Johnny and Indra entered the house. The dark corridor led them to a living room. And there he was, tall and pale, with blazing red eyes, a choir of dark murmurs following his presence. Dominic was sitting at the end of a long, narrow table. He was wearing a black suit from the 18th century and playing with a fork and knife over a piece of turkey. Lara sat at the opposite end.

"What the fuck is she doing here?!" Johnny blurted out as he ran towards her. Shadows from the candles aligned on the table and danced over her cloudy face as she ran her fingers through her disheveled hair. Her hands were quivering and her elegant red dress was thorn and dirty.

"Good evening," Dominic said. "Forgive me for not standing up. But considering the circumstances, I believe my manners are not of great importance."

"Lara," Johnny leaned over and gently cupped her cheek, "What happened?"

"Nothing," she mumbled.

Johnny embraced her, his hands shaking, his voice quivering. "Tell me what happened."

"Nothing," she almost cried. She took his hand, lifted her head to look him straight in the eyes, and repeated, "Nothing happened."

"This is not how you told me it would be," Indra said. "Your messenger said you found a loophole."

"The loophole!" Dominic yelled. "An old Egyptian necklace that can break any curse if carried on the night when the seven far stars align? Our handsome writer here wanted me to use it so he could show how pathetic people can be when they are truly in love and what nonsense they will believe in to preserve hope. I can carry it for the rest of eternity and nothing is going to change. Instead I am going to keep killing you, just like before. This isn't Vampire Diaries or Originals. Our creator is a dark psychopath who imagined a quote on the back cover of his book. A quote that says 'Hope is the most important ingredient of hell.'"

"It will work. You need to have faith!" Indra said.

"It will not. I spoke with Johnny's girl. She knows everything about his manuscripts. Even his other stories, Never Mind the Sun is destined to be a tragedy. An everlasting hell for two souls in love," Dominic replied.

"I refuse to believe that. I believe the necklace is our salvation!" Indra objected.

"If his necklace had enough strength to destroy the curse, that would make it more powerful than I am. And my magic wouldn't be able to destroy it. But look." He raised the golden necklace with a red jewel in its middle and melted it in his palm.

The golden-red streamlet trickled to the floor. Smoke rose above it as Indra looked down.

"However, I have found a loophole," Dominic added. "The writer needs to suffer and see what the two of us are going through. That is the only loophole. If he doesn't change his manuscripts, our suffering will end only with his death."

"There must be another way," Indra mumbled.

A painful moan escaped Lara and a few tears slid over her face. Then she went quiet.

"What did you do to her?" Johnny yelled, slamming his fist on the table.

The food and candles shook. A potato rolled from a plate and fell to the floor.

"I wanted to play… She didn't… But I was just too playful, so I made her play," he said.

"He didn't. Everything is fine," Lara chimed up.

"You son of a bitch!" Johnny rushed towards Dominic.

Though in vain, he swung his one fist with all his might. Dominic's strength was out of this world. Effortlessly, he caught the writer's fist and squeezed it. The writer screamed. Lara and Indra jumped in and attempted to pull Dominic away, but his body was a statue made of stone. When he released him, Johnny's arm was completely numb.

"Sit," Dominic ordered.

Lara returned to her seat while Johnny and Indra took the middle seats across from each other.

"You lured me here," Johnny told Indra, his eyes filled with rage.

"I didn't! I swear to God I didn't know this was going to happen! He told me he found a loophole in your story! He said we would finally be able to stop the killing!" Indra claimed.

"Please… Help yourselves," Dominic said. "The turkey is still hot."

"What the fuck is this? Thanksgiving?" Johnny asked disdainfully.

"It wouldn't hurt to show a little gratitude for what we have, would it now?" Dominic retorted.

"Let her go!" Johnny threatened.

"Or what?" Dominic looked at him insolently.

Silence fell over the table.

The writer was the one to break it. "Lara. Look at me. Tell me the name of our song."

"When I dream," Lara answered, confused.

"No… I wrote that in the book. Tell me, what do you call the first drops of sperm?"

"Johnny…? What the fuck is wrong with you?" Lara yelled.

"Please! It's important. What do you call the drops of sperm that spurt from the cock before a man comes?"

"I don't call it anyhow." Lara sighed.

"Love tears? Does that ring a bell?" he asked.

"What fucking love tears?" she hissed.

"Thank you, God!" Johnny exclaimed with great relief. "You are only a character. For a moment, I thought you were real."

"You consider the products of your writing worthless?" Dominic inquired. "No wonder you can't hit the bestseller."

"I love what I write. But I am one of those guys who regards the welfare of real people more important than the well-being of book characters," Johnny replied. "But I guess you will never know what that means…"

"What the fuck are you two going on about?" Lara interfered.

"The writer was checking for discrepancies between the muse and the character. And now he feels relief because he knows you are from his book, Stories from the Brothel, am I right? Otherwise, you would know something from his life he omitted to write," Dominic explained.

"I know he wrote about me," Lara said.

She was barely holding onto her fork and knife. Johnny thought she might be drugged.

"That's not what I said. You are not the muse. You are the character inspired by the muse," Dominic clarified.

"Now listen!" Johnny exclaimed. "I don't want to take this shit anymore. Either kill me, or I return to Babylon and fuck my brains out until this condition in my head passes. Then I will go to the bridge and do what you want to do."

"Well," Dominic took a sip of wine, "I would like to have my vengeance."

"Then fucking do it!" Johnny hissed.

"I will."

"Dominic!" Indra shouted. "You promised! This is not the way!"

"I thought of breaking your spine," he started, "But that would only leave you paralyzed. You wouldn't feel pain while I break your other bones. Then I thought of smashing your arms and legs under a great weight. But that would prevent you from feeling agony. True suffering has nothing to do with the pain of flesh and bones. So, I decided that Lara was the best choice," Dominic concluded.

His body merged with the shadows. He disappeared and in the blink of an eye, after a gust of wind swayed the candle flames, appeared behind Lara. His lips were parted, his upper fangs jutting halfway down his chin.

"Dominic!" Indra yelled.

Lara turned around and faced the bloodthirsty apparition. She didn't show any fear, which was exactly how the real Lara would react. She would make a fuss about an imaginary eye exchange with another woman but calmly go into the basement to hide from a sky filled with explosions.

Lara stared at him serenely. Johnny remained sitting, supposedly calm, in a vain attempt to hide his disquiet. He knew Dominic could hear and feel his heartbeats.

"All right!" Johnny jumped in. "Leave her the fuck alone!"

"Why?" Dominic asked with surprise on his face. "She is only a character?"

"I don't want you to ruin my work," Johnny answered.

"I believe there is something more to it." He put both palms around Lara's neck. As he began to squeeze, she began grunting.

"Dominic! Let her go!" Indra yelled.

"Leave her alone!" Johnny roared.

"Again? Or what?" Dominic pierced the writer with his red eyes. "What are you going to do about it?"

"I will postpone my suicide. Wash dishes! Collect garbage! Clean toilets and dive into sewers to save money for high-quality promotions and make sure Never Mind the Sun reaches as many readers as possible," Johnny threatened.

"Oh? I am shit scared," Dominic provoked.

"That isn't the end of it. I am going to change the book!" Johnny continued.

"Oh, really?"

"I will force you to kill all your future children and eat their hearts for eternity. You will live in infinite torment without ever knowing the reason for your fate," Johnny finished.

"That is my life already," the cursed vampire retorted as he pulled Lara to her feet.

Then Johnny rushed at him, but Dominic and Lara merged into the shadows. Passing through the ceiling, they rose to the second floor of the house. Indra and Johnny ran to the stairs. Halfway up, they heard a shriek. Johnny froze and fell back, but Indra pushed him up. The writer's heart was hammering in his chest as he raced up the stairs. On the second floor there were several doors in a narrow passage.

Johnny ran into the first room, but there was no one there. Returning to the corridor, he saw an opened door from the room across. With fear streaming through his spine, Johnny approached.

Indra was standing next to a big oak bed with a canopy and see-through red curtains falling from above. On the wall to the left, in red color, stood the lines, "Over and there, by Bilbo Baggins. Or maybe not."

Johnny stepped forward and spotted a trunk-shaped mass protruding under a blanket.

"I swear to God, I didn't know this was going to happen," Indra said.

"What's under the blanket?" Johnny shouted, trembling. He would start toward the bed, only to cower back the very next moment. His face twitched, his chin quivering.

"You don't have to see this," she said.

"Is it what I think it is!" Johnny screamed

Indra looked down. "I am so sorry," she whispered.

"Oh, fuck!" Johnny bent and barely managed not to throw up.

He started crying. Tears were running down his face as he approached the bed. Throughout centuries, Dominic engaged in massacres, consumed with rage after killing Indra. Turned entire villages and cities into slaughterhouses.

"Don't do it!" Indra said.

"I must."

As he reached for the curtain, a red drop fell onto his shoulder. Johnny turned his head. The drop was big and slowly soaked into the cotton of his elegant jacket. Another drop fell after the first.

"Don't look up," Indra said.

"What is up there?" Johnny asked.

He lifted his head slowly, but Indra rushed to him, cupped his face, and pulled it down.

"What is up there?" Johnny repeated.

"She is not real! She is from your book," Indra said.

A red streamlet dropped on his shoulder and slid down his sleeve.

"Please don't!" said Indra, but he was already looking up.

Lara's limbs were all over the ceiling. They were impaled to the wall through her bones. Her face and torso were nowhere to be seen. That had to mean, the thought rushed through Johnny's mind, that the rest is under the blanket. He began panting, his face turning pale as mortar. He couldn't make a sound. Indra pushed him out. As he was going backward through the door, he noticed the lines on the wall had changed. Now it said, "I am going for the muse."

"He is going for the real Lara!" Johnny shouted.

"Calm down!" she said.

Johnny fumbled in his pockets. He pulled out his phone and dialed the real Lara. She answered after the fifth ring.

"Hello, my Johnny! My pretty Johnny! I was just going to sleep," she said in a tired, mischievous voice.

"Lara!" he yelled. "Listen! It's urgent! I might be going insane, but a powerful vampire may be headed toward you. You must hide! But there might not be a vampire. It could be me. I might be going towards you, thinking that I am the vampire who wants to kill you. Don't open your door to anyone! And don't believe anything that I tell you."

"Johnny, you are high! I am going to sleep. Goodbye!" Lara hung up.

He called again, but she didn't answer. He knew she had gone into silent mode. Johnny was twitching his head and raking his hair with his fingers.

"He can't harm her! This is all in my head!"

Indra looked at him mutely.

"Why are you looking at me like that?" Johnny shouted.

"He is powerful!" she mumbled.

"But this is only happening in my head?! Right? This can't be really happening?" He stared at Indra desperately.

"You tell me," she said.

"Oh, fuck! Oh, fuck!" Like a mad fly, Johnny buzzed through the corridor.

"You need to calm down," she said.

"I need to stop him!"

He came up with a plan.

"I will kill myself. Right now!" he loudly announced his decision and approached the stairs, preparing to jump on his head. "When I am gone, he too will cease to exist."

"You might not kill yourself. You could break your neck and stay paralyzed," Indra pointed out. "In that case, you would only suffer while Lara would still…"

"Fuck! You are right," he hissed. "Rope? Do you have a rope?" Johnny blurted out.

Getting no response, he started running from one room to another. Indra chased after the writer, trying unsuccessfully to stop him. But he behaved like she didn't exist. There was no rope. And since his brain was muddled, Johnny failed to see the bed sheets or curtains as a worthy substitute to hang himself from the balustrade, if it was strong enough not to break.

He strode downstairs and took the carving knife from the dining table. When the blade touched his neck, he realized it wouldn't be sharp enough. He then took a crystal goblet and smashed it on the floor where he picked the sharpest piece of glass and rested it against his neck artery.

"Wait!" Indra shouted.

Johnny looked at her, his eyes full of fear and desperation. He was panting like a dog, his face drenched in sweat.

"There is nothing else to do!"

"What will happen to Lara if you kill yourself?" Indra asked.

His face crumpled.

"I don't understand you. What does Lara…?"

"You just talked to real Lara," Indra pointed out. "If you kill yourself, she will blame herself for hanging up on you for the rest of her life. Do you want her to live with that guilt?"

After a momentary silence, Johnny chuckled and said, "I don't think she gives a fuck."

"Oh, but she does. And so do you," Indra said. "Otherwise you wouldn't have that smile all over your face."

"Don't be silly," he replied, smiling.

"But I am not," Indra said. "Somethings I know. Some-things I don't. But I sure can recognize a man in love."

"There is no love," the writer retorted.

"Oh, but there is. Love is the only force capable of making such a selfish piece of shit like you forget his wishes and think about the welfare of another being," Indra replied. "You love her. And she loves you. The way she answered your call…"

"Nah! She likes luxury as much as I do… Without money, the two of us would depart faster than we fucked. And even if we wouldn't, she is fifteen years older than me. Soon, she will start withering, becoming ugly. And I would return to the prostitutes."

"If you say so," Indra said before adding, "But you know what I think? I think you would love her even if she was the oldest woman in the world."

The shard of glass was still pressing against his artery, but his hand wasn't so sure anymore. His lips lifted into a wide grin.

"So what do you suggest?" the writer yelled. "Dominic might have already found her."

"He didn't. Dominic isn't sure what she looks like. Nor does he know where she lives. You masked everything in your book. Yes, you used her real name, but there are millions of Laras in this world."

"He can turn into shadows! He could kill all the red-haired Laras of this world in one night," Johnny yelled.

Indra was silent for a few moments before she exclaimed, "I think there is something we can do… Where is your orig-inal Never Mind the Sun manuscript?"

"I left it in the trailer," the writer whispered.

"You could strip Dominic of his powers there," she said.

"I will change the fucking end in any way he wants! He just needs to leave Lara alone!" Johnny shouted. He squeezed the piece of glass and blood trickled from his palm. "I will give him heaven. The two of you. Happy forever! Is that what you wanted the entire time!?" Johnny threw the bloody piece of glass at the wall.

"I swear I didn't know it would be like this," Indra said.

"You get what you wanted!" Johnny hissed.

They rushed from the house and barged into the Bentley. Ron stepped on the gas and the car started towards Johnny's residence.

7

They arrived at the bridge. Ron stopped the car at the exact place where Johnny had intended to jump. The writer strode out and rushed to the stairs. Ron trailed behind him.

Indra took over the wheel and stepped on the gas. She headed to Lara's place. The address Johnny gave her was an hour away. She had to drive as fast as possible and reach Lara before Dominic. She needed to tell him the manuscript is being changed. But the end of the century was nearing. Indra knew his urges could overwhelm him at any moment. And if that happens, he would kill everyone who crosses his path regardless of what they tell him. It could have happened in the house. But Indra had to try to give Johnny time to change the manuscript and take the powers from his cursed vampire.

When the writer reached the bottom of the stairs, Ron was not even halfway down. The road to his trailer was dark. Only a few of the streetlights were working. Hundreds of faces peered from the shadows. All were familiar. Angels, demons, and psychopaths. They were still and watching him pass. Their eyes glimmered like fallen stars dispersed over the dark wasteland.

Johnny made his first step, the crowd murmuring. He paid them attention and found that they were speaking about their desires. The writer continued forward, barely distinguishing the silhouette of his body from the darkness when something gripped his wrist. He jerked his arm and broke free. Hands began clawing at his chest and shoulders. The whispers turned into coherent words.

"I want my son to be the youngest wrestling champion in the world!"

"I want to be prettier than my sister!"

"Can you give me arms and legs, please?"

Johnny swung his arms and elbows in all directions. As he neared the first illuminated streetlight, the apparitions' numbers started to decrease. When he reached the light, there was no one. All of them were lurking and whispering in the darkness. The streetlight blinked, a sudden gust of wind, and the writer felt the cold in his bones as he rushed forward, and as soon as he left the circle of light, he felt his characters reaching for him. When he dove into the darkness, he heard their desires clearly.

"I want my uncle to die! I don't want him to abuse me anymore!"

"Give me money for my child's therapy!"

"Let me win the lottery! I was not born for this here poverty!"

Johnny screamed and went on swinging his hands like a madman. There were too many of them. Too many desires. Too many mouths speaking at the same time. As he made his way through the crowd, Johnny heard a shout, "He has a knife!" A second later, he saw a sharp rectangle shining above his head. But then someone stood between it and him and took the blade. Johnny could not see who it was, for the darkness was impenetrable. There were only eyes gleaming like fireflies. He heard the grunting and coughing.

"Hold him!"

"He will die!"

"What is his last wish?"

"I wanted to kill God," the dying man grunted.

The writer rushed forward and made his way to the next street light. He was more than halfway through the throngs. He ran straight into the night and strode through the desires of thousands.

"I don't want to turn forty and remain a virgin! Can you pump me up?"

"I need to find my father's will or my brother will take everything!"

"I don't know who I am!? I have amnesia? Can you help me remember?"

Johnny dived toward the last light. It was over the lawn around his trailer. He could hear his dog barking. When Johnny reached that light, he found that he was not alone. A blurry apparition was standing under the street lamp. When the fogginess cleared, Johnny saw it was a pregnant woman. But not just any pregnant woman. It was Akira from "A Hundred Years of Pregnancy." Her pregnancy had lasted thirty years. She was almost fifty and still in what seemed like her eighth month, still throwing up and having mood changes every half an hour or so.

"Can you make my pregnancy end?" she asked.

Sweat was running down her red, round face. She wiped her forehead with her swollen fingers.

"I…"

"Could you please grant me only that one wish? I don't think I ask much."

Johnny sighed deeply. "I can't."

"But why? I just want my pregnancy to finally end."

"If all of the characters' desires are fulfilled, no book could ever be written," the writer replied. "If your pregnancy lasts only nine months, then there would be no novel. I mean, who would want to read about a happily pregnant woman? Happiness is boring. And a reader has no bigger adversary than boredom. Fear and laziness are a kindergarten of unpleasantness when compared to being bored."

"So, I have to carry a child for thirty years for the amusement of some reader?" she asked.

Johnny was silent.

"I don't even know if I am going to ever give birth or carry it in my womb for another thirty years?" she looked at him desperately.

"I thought…" the writer stopped.

"Say it!" she hissed.

"I was thinking that you would die before giving birth. In old age. Or giving birth to a dead born after fifty years. The baby would be born alive but could choke on their navel cord because of the doctor's incompetency," he explained.

"But why?"

"I've told you," he said. "I wanted to create a story to impress my readers."

They looked at each other in silence. Johnny strode into the darkness. This time, the crowd was wilder. They didn't whisper their desires. They were giving vent to their rage instead. Fists and palms rained down on the writer. They were pulling him from one side to the other, their grips growing stronger. They wanted to tear him apart.

"What are we? Your slaves?"

"Are we only toys for you to play with? To play and impress others?"

"Selling our lives trapped in papers between circus covers and making us relive our sufferings as many times as someone reads about us!"

They overpowered him and he fell to the ground. They were kicking and stomping him. Johnny was on the brink of passing out, but something pulled him forward right before the dark curtains fell over his eyes. When he came around, Johnny saw that his savior was a dog. He was swinging his tail and barking, Johnny's face wet from the dog's saliva. He got up and barged into the trailer.

The writer dropped to his knees and peered under the bed, only to see layers of dust everywhere. He ran to the closet. Johnny pulled out all his clothes and turned them inside out, including the socks, despite knowing that the story was in a big notebook with a hard cover that could hardly be folded, let alone shoved inside a sock. "Never Mind the Sun" was like all of the manuscripts Johnny wrote on paper before typing it up on his laptop.

After the closet, he looked in all the kitchen cabinets, even in the toilet cistern. Rushing back to the kitchen, Johnny found a knife, pulled the mattress from the bed, and sliced it in the middle. He shoved his fingers deep inside the sponge and tore it piece by piece until deep inside he stumbled upon a notebook. Hardcover, red.

But it was not "Never Mind the Sun." He was holding a parody called "Remember When Love Was Red?" It was a story about a virgin girl who wanted to have sex only with the man who would make her pregnant. The writer had turned the trailer upside down and inside out, but couldn't find the right notebook.

"What you are looking for is looking for you, too. But it can't recognize you because of a disturbance." A gentle female voice sounded from the sofa.

The back of someone's head with long smooth hair the color of soil was visible above the backrest. It was bathing in the light coming from the glimmering circle on the ceiling.

"Come here. Look at me," she said.

Johnny circled the sofa.

"Don't you recognize me?" her voice echoed.

"Jesus?" Johnny asked in disbelief.

"Who did you expect it to be in the time of your biggest need?" she inquired.

Johnny took a better look and realized it really was his Jesus from "Heaven Can Wait." He had written a book about the third savior coming as a woman, hoping to gain popularity amongst feminists. But that didn't turn too well and his novel didn't even sell the first run of two thousand copies.

"Yes... Well, after everything that has happened tonight, Jesus' arrival sure comes as no surprise," Ron remarked as he entered the trailer.

"You need to allow yourself to find the manuscript," Jesus said.

Just then, Johnny's phone rang.

"Johnny?" Lara's voice was quivering. "There is a strange man in front of my house. He is standing in the shadows under the tree across the street and staring at my window."

"Fuck!"

"And then he goes away. As in he almost vanishes. And then he comes back. I tried calling the police, but the call won't go through. I don't know what to do," she said.

"Are you alone in the house?" Johnny asked.

"Yes. I locked all the doors and windows. I am kneeling next to my window and peaking between the curtains. I don't think he can see me. I..."

The connection broke. Johnny called her back, but Lara was unavailable.

"This is real! Fuck!"

"You need to calm down," Jesus said.

"How am I supposed to calm down when he is going to kill the only woman I have ever loved?" Johnny yelled, trying to call Lara again. "And the manuscript is lost!"

"All lost things can be found. All broken things can be fixed. And everything that was ever destroyed can be resurrected," Jesus assured him. "But for that to happen, you first need to achieve peace."

The writer would not find peace. Not even for a moment. He buzzed around his trailer like a mad fly and once again turned his tiny home upside down. He picked up and looked under every object in the trailer, big and small, flat or round. He checked every pocket. Poured the sugar, coffee, and salt out of their cups just in case the notebook was hidden in there. He pulled the toilet seat from the floor in case he had accidentally flushed the manuscript.

Only when he had broken the toilet seat did desperation finally overwhelm him. Johnny fell to his knees in front of Jesus and lifted his palms, praying, his face distorted, sobs escaping his mouth. There were no tears. Then it stopped. He went silent and his head fell to Jesus's knees.

And there, under her foot, was an old green notebook that Johnny somehow failed to spot.

"Oh my God!? Is that it?"

"You need to learn to let go," she replied.

"Thank you," Johnny said.

When Johnny grabbed at the notebook, he couldn't pick it up. The writer looked up at Jesus in confusion and tried again to pull it up. Her foot was like a pillar. Silence fell.

The writer mumbled, "Jesus, what are you doing?"

"I want to be pure," she said. "I don't want all this filth inside me."

Johnny frowned with disbelief.

"Even you?" he shouted.

"What did you expect?" Jesus asked. "You made me. Life is hard enough. Shit stinks and we have to wipe our asses. Not to mention diseases, poverty, rapes, murders, and all the other shit that has nothing to do with our digestion."

"What do you want?!" Johnny asked desperately.

"You know what I want," she replied.

He chuckled. "You want never to have to shit, piss, or bleed?"

"Swear to me," Jesus said.

"Swear to you what?"

"For money. You will never become rich if you don't give me what I asked for," she said. "Swear to me and I will let you have your manuscript."

"I fucking swear!" the writer roared. Instantly, Jesus perished into the light.

Johnny took the notebook, grabbed the first pen he saw, and wrote on the first page, "Dominic doesn't have any powers. He imagined everything you are about to read. He never hurt a fly, let alone a human being. Dominic was a man who suffered from clinical delusions. Eventually they pass and leave him as normal as a man can be. Indra and Dominic can choose to live if they please."

"There!" Johnny yelled. "It's done. You have your happily ever after, you Bastard."

His cell phone rang. It was Lara.

"I will rip her to pieces," he heard Dominic say. Shrieks echoed in the background.

"I changed it. You got your happily ever after!" Johnny yelled as the connection broke. "I changed it. I gave him a happily ever after! You got a happily ever after!"

He jumped and crumpled the manuscript. Ron rushed over and delivered his best hook to the writer's head. Johnny fell like a sack of potatoes on the sofa.

"Be a man!" Ron roared. "Once in your life, be a man!"

"I changed it! I changed it! Why does he want to kill her?" Johnny mumbled. His face turned red, veins popping out of his forehead.

"You changed it? Scribbling a few more lines at the beginning and the end is not a change. That is shit," Ron yelled.

"But he is going to kill her! Look," Johnny pointed through the window. The blush of dawn was spreading across the sky, the clouds clearing up and the first light falling over the bridge. And there, right in the middle, a Bentley had stopped, its door opened. It was not Indra who came out. It was Dominic.

"Oh fuck! This isn't good!" Ron muttered and rushed out.

Johnny picked the manuscript from the floor and followed him. The road wasn't dark anymore, but all his characters were still there. They were standing at the sides of the road. Their presence made Johnny laugh while he ran. They truly were, the writer admitted, one big sad company of errors. In the light of dawn, Ron seemed bigger. He was like a locomotive running out of coal, his face red and wet. The big guy was barely breathing and his lungs wheezed with every breath. Somewhere halfway down the road, a coughing fit made him double over.

Somehow, despite all the coughing, he kept going. A little before they reached the last of the stairs, Ron fell. He was hyperventilating, his chest heaving like a balloon in the mouth of a clumsy child, his round face drenched in sweat and red as blood.

Johnny bent over. Ron's two muscular hands could hardly grip the lapel of his elegant jacket. He was trying to say something, but his words were cut in half. Johnny kneeled and cupped Ron's face with his palms.

"C… C…c…c…c… Can…?" Ron just couldn't get a word right.

"Yes," Johnny said. "Jenny will go to Harvard! I promise."

Ron's lips lifted into an arc. His eyes remained open and his chest stopped moving. Ron lay as still as a fallen statue. Johnny knew it was a heart attack. Ron was born with a flaw the doctors had failed to see. He had a hole in his heart that could kill him at any moment. Ron had found out about the flaw when the army rejected him. He had failed their medical exams. He had told no one except Oliver.

Johnny gently pressed his lips to Ron's forehead and kissed him. "She will be the best in her class," he whispered before jumping to his feet and rushing up the stairs. Reaching the top, he saw Dominic. The cursed vampire was standing in the middle of the bridge, his lost gaze piercing the river. His eyes weren't blazing anymore. They were dark and dead. Dawn's rays cradled his pale face. As Johnny approached him, he saw something bloody in his palm. It was a heart. Indra's heart, the writer knew right away. It was still beating.

"I released you!" he screamed, waving the manuscript. "I released you from your curse!"

Dominic said nothing. Johnny ran to him.

"Where is Lara? Where is she?" he asked with desperation in his eyes.

There was no reply.

"Did you hurt her? Tell me!" Johnny dropped the manuscript and grabbed the lapels of Dominic's jacket. The vampire shook. He wasn't a statue anymore. Now, he was mortal, with no powers to fight back. Just an ordinary pale slender man.

"I could have given you anything you want. Anything! You only needed to say what. Tell me where she is!" the writer roared.

"She will be fine," Dominic muttered. "I could not hurt her even if I wanted… All this is only in your head."

The writer backed down.

"Only in my head," he chuckled.

"But your word is my world. Your thoughts are all that we have," Dominic said.

"I changed everything. I released you from your curse and gave you the happily ever after," Johnny told him.

"I killed Indra." Dominic said as he lifted his other hand, a big bloody knife shaking in his fist.

"I changed the manuscript," Johnny repeated in shock and confusion. "The curse is broken."

"I know." Dominic said as he looked down. "I carved her heart out with this knife. You weren't specific enough with your change. Nowhere in your new script did you say I would never kill Indra. You only said I imagined everything."

"I was under pressure. I gave you a choice. I gave you a life of choices. You could have chosen anything you wanted."

"Choices can be curses."

"What?" the writer asked. "But why did you have to kill her?"

"It was in me the entire time," Dominic admitted. "The urge I didn't know existed. The urge hidden deep inside the very core of my existence. My entire life, I blamed you. I blamed the curse. But it was me all along."

"That is not true. I made you all those things," the writer said.

Dominic looked at him. A few tears ran from his dark eyes. He waved his arm and the heart flew into the river.

"You are good," the vampire said, as the sun danced over his face. "Never Mind the Sun."

"I can change it. I can change the book," Johnny pleaded.

"What's done is done. Nobody needs to change. What people need is salvation. A place where everyone will be accepted and loved. Can you imagine it?"

"I can't," Johnny admitted.

Dominic swung the knife into the river and threw one leg over the railing.

"You could write a book about it. Who knows…?" the now ex-vamp suggested. "But you need a good title. What could we call it?"

"What are you doing?" the writer asked.

"I am mortal now, am I not?" Dominic asked as he flung his other leg over the railing.

"Yes, you are," Johnny said.

"It feels good to be final," Dominic said. "From the perspective of tormenting immortality, the ability to die is a great power. Death is the deity of immortality."

"Changes are good," Johnny said. "Even from life to death."

"Heaven for everyone," Dominic said, his lips widening into a smile.

"What?" Johnny asked.

Instead of a reply, he got to witness Dominic's fall.

The body got smaller and smaller until it disappeared in the foam from the clash. Then he was gone. Johnny remained on the bridge for a while. His characters around him retreated. Some followed and dived into the river without returning to the surface. Others stepped out into the neverending wasteland and began diminishing until they became dots that merged with the horizon.

"I guess this is the end of my head trauma," the writer muttered to himself, climbing down the stairs.

He walked back to his trailer and fainted on the bed.

8

The sound of knocking woke him. Johnny got up from his ripped sponge, tripped on the chair lying on its side, barely reaching the door in one piece. Through the small curtains, he saw a woman in a short black dress and shoes with open-toe high heels, similar to the ones Kayla had been wearing his last night. He wouldn't mind if the head trauma lasted a little longer, long enough for another fuck like the last one.

When he opened the door, he saw her red hair. It was Lara.

"Hey Johnny," she smiled and entered.

"What in the name of God happened here?" she asked in shock when she saw the upturned room.

"I had the craziest day in my life," he admitted.

"I can see that," she said. "You frightened me last night, you know? And, God, when that guy appeared!"

"How did he look?" Johnny asked excitedly. "Was he tall and pale, like a vampire? With red eyes?"

"No," Lara chuckled. "He wasn't like a vampire. It was a little fat man with red cheeks. After the connection broke, he entered my yard, took his dick out, and started jerking. But the police picked him up in a matter of minutes. It was some retarded person who had just escaped from the madhouse."

"Thank God," Johnny exhaled with great relief. "That gives me the idea for the best book ever."

"Oh, really?" Lara looked at him mischievously.

"Yes. The title is…"

"What is a gun doing here?" Lara interrupted him.

And there it was—a shiny gun lying beside the sofa.

Before Johnny managed to say anything, she slapped him.

"What was that for?" Johnny yelled in disbelief.

"If I wasn't wearing this brand new dress, I would beat the fuck out of you!" she shouted back. Her frowning face turned red, piercing Johnny with her gaze.

"I don't understand."

"Listen to me! We've had this conversation so many damn times. You will make it! But don't start with that suicidal shit because you don't have enough money to orgy with your whores and all the perversions that you want to do!"

"Lara?"

"I don't want to hear about it. I know it's hard. I know you are "not made for this life of poverty." I believe in you. Your mother believes in you. Imagine how she would feel if you were gone."

Johnny looked down.

"Did you, at least for a moment, stop to think about what your suicide would do to your mother?"

"I didn't. But everything is so... I..."

"You will make it," she interrupted him. "Your books will find their way to high-quality publishers and you will earn tons of money. But you need to be patient," she said and settled on the sofa.

Johnny sat next to her. She crossed her legs and her fluttery dress climbed up her smooth thighs. She dangled one foot, making the shoe occasionally touch her heel and sole. Shiny red polish covered her nails. The air was hot and heavy. Being this close to Lara was enough to give him a hard-on.

She gripped his wrist as she always did and asked, "Now, what's with this new book that you mentioned?"

"Heaven for Everyone," Johnny replied. "That's its title."

Her hand glided from his elbow to his shoulder. "It sounds incredible," she said. "The title is completely mad."

She lifted her leg even more, so the shoe hung only by the thin black strap. Then Lara twitched her foot. The shoe fell on the floor and her bare foot remained in the air, hovering.

"Do you like my nails?" she asked as she moved her foot onto his lap. "I did them this morning."

"I love them," Johnny replied.

Lara kicked off the other shoe. "Tell me more about this Heaven for Everyone," she said.

After only a few words explaining his plan for the story, Lara mounted him. Her tongue pushed into his mouth shutting him up. Her kiss turned into an attempt to devour him.

Like unrestrained animals, their tongues wrestled in their mouths, their bodies firmly rubbing each other.

Johnny rolled Lara on her back and settled between her legs. He impaled her on his cock and slowly started moving his hips. Lara pushed him back and put her feet on his face. One sole rested on his cheek while the toes of the other foot dived deep inside his mouth. She banged the back of his throat. After pulling her foot out, Lara smeared all the saliva from her toes over the writer's face. Johnny was straining his groin and pinching his balls as hard as he could to prevent himself from coming.

"Come down," Lara moaned.

She spread her legs wider and put her hands on his shoulders, pulling him down, their bodies merging. Lara stuck out her tongue and ran it all over his face.

"Lick my face," she moaned.

Johnny's tongue glided over her cheeks. Their faces became slippery. Lara was groaning, her cunt contracting. Then they stopped and remained still. Johnny was lying over her. His head was leaning against hers, warm air circulating between their open mouths, their breaths colliding, harmonized. His exhale became her inhale and the other way around.

"Look at me," she said.

Johnny stared into her dark green eyes. There was nothing but impudence in them. In the garden of her soul, the apple was still an untasted fruit. Shame was hiding in the bushes, too shy to come into the open, but the fall was near.

She was a woman in the biblical sense of the word, a whore from the Old Testimony. She made men believe they were flying, and only after the crash would they realize they were falling.

"Fill me," she moaned. "I have a copper coil in my cunt."

He pushed hard, their groins colliding loudly. Johnny's cock spewed his progeny deep inside Lara's crack. Her cunt was full of the writer's offspring and her coil served them the copper. Johnny remained in her. They remained lying in silence for some time. Then Lara told him that her ex-husband had gotten into some serious business with cocaine and had promised her big money if she helped.

"When I become rich," she concluded, "you will not have to worry about anything."

"I just hope this book brings me what I want," Johnny said ignoring the whole cocaine thing.

Instead he told Lara all about his previous day and night. The entire story. And then he told her about his idea for the book in which all his characters get salvation.

"Heaven for Everyone sounds like a perfect title," Lara agreed.

But her voice was crisp and her gaze filled with dissatisfaction.

"You are lucky to be alive. Guns don't backfire often," she said. "And I am furious with you. Furious."

"Listen… just forget it," Johnny suggested.

"I don't want to forget it. You are a friend. I love you and want you to succeed. But you have to fight," she said.

He pulled his dick out of her and moved back.

"I can't work from nine to five. No, I just can't! Nor can I stand the people there! I can't stand an office! Or the idea of a low salary! I can't stand it! I can't stand it for my fucking life!" he hissed. "And the most terrible thing is I can't write when I work. I have tried. But after eight hours of dish-washing, packet hauling, or diving into the paperwork, I can't write a coherent fucking sentence."

Lara sighed as if her lungs were forced to lift a heavy burden. "Then what are you going to do?"

"I will give myself a shot with Heaven for Everyone. One last shot," he replied.

"Simon wants to marry me," she said.

"Marry him," Johnny said. "You will be a millionairess."

"I can't stand him!"

"He lets you do whatever you wish. He lets you fuck whomever you want. And he gives you money. Simon is a fairy-tale prince." Johnny thought for a moment. "No. Not a prince. A king from a fairy tale."

"I can't stand him! I will help my ex to sell the white powder and get me my money."

"What makes you think he will give you anything?" Johnny asked.

"I raised our two children. Not once did I sue him or nag about the money. He remembers that," she said. "He can trust me."

"You told me he has a new younger girlfriend. And you know how things are with older men and young girls…"

"I don't want to think about that."

"I hope you are right," Johnny said.

"I am also in a relationship with Edin again," Lara confessed.

"Oh, my God! You are insane."

"I know."

"You are both insane. Edin will never change. He will beat you again. Maybe even kill you."

"This is his last chance," Lara said.

"You've said that the last five times," Johnny pointed out.

"But it's love."

"It's not love. You are incapable of love."

"Edin thinks so, too," Lara admitted.

"If you truly loved him, you wouldn't be fucking me here now."

"That's what friends do for each other." Lara smiled mischievously.

Johnny chuckled, "I wasn't talking only about you. I think people are incapable of love."

"Oh, come on…"

"No, listen. Women are like the wind. Regardless of how strong you blow, you can disappear or change direction in the blink of an eye. Men, on the other hand, are like locomotives. We need time to get on the track and increase our speed. And we need a tremendous amount of force to step on the brake and stop," Johnny explained. "I have a great breaking force. With me, you don't have to worry. But Edin? God, he is fucked up in his head. I think someone is going to kill you…"

"If only you were seven years older," she said.

"Here we go again," Johnny grumbled.

"A fifteen years age difference is simply too much. I am too old for you."

"Luckily for me, when it comes to mental age, you behave like a child."

Her phone rang. It was Edin. They were supposed to be meeting at a downtown restaurant.

"I have to go," Lara said and stood up from the sofa.

Before leaving, she took out a big wad of money from her bag and threw it all over Johnny. His face split into a wide smile as the bills fell over him.

"From my ex. I know what kind of rain you like," Lara said with a raunchy smile. "You will have to put some effort into picking them up though."

"I love you too," Johnny said.

He stood up and hugged her. They pressed against each other as if they wanted to enter the other's body. But they needed even more strength to hold their eyes closed. Deep breaths went hand in hand. They were a whole. When she was there, Johnny felt like nothing bad could happen, not only to him but to anyone else in the world.

"Remember when we first met?" she asked with her mouth on the base of his neck.

"Of course, I do," he said. "You are the only pretty girl I never had to pay."

Lara chuckled. "And you are the only man who planned to marry me for my money."

"Which, unfortunately, as it turned out, you didn't have."

Their lips embraced each other in a quick kiss.

"I have to go now," Lara said. But she turned at the door. "Johnny, you know you can call me anytime you want?"

"I know."

"If the idea to harm yourself in any way ever crosses your mind, promise me you will call."

"I promise," he replied.

She sent him a kiss and left.

Johnny dug out the laptop from under his bed and started writing.

9

Johnny started with the conjoined twins, Jim and Jack. They had two heads and necks but shared one body. Those were the guys who had chased them in the limo while they were driving to meet with Dominic.

As Johnny had explained to Indra, they had fallen in love with the same prostitute. One day, the brothers engaged in a fight. Jack controlled the right arm, which was stronger than the left belonging to Jim. However, Jim had a longer and fully functional neck, which allowed him to deliver head punches. At some point, Jack grabbed Jim's throat and strangled him. Sadly, Jim's brain controlled erections so Jack couldn't fuck the love of his life.

Johnny granted Jack a quick death and sent the twins to heaven as normal twin brothers. Then he turned the prostitute into two pretty twin sisters who wanted nothing more but to please the brothers. The sisters even engaged in sex fights as foreplay and often switched brothers to refresh their lovemaking.

As for the pregnant woman, Johnny decided she was going to become the goddess of fertility. After she died giving birth to a healthy young boy, she went to heaven. There she watched over her son who became the president of the new-age government and had three daughters. He lived happily and died in his sleep.

The warden didn't eat his wives anymore. Both Lilith, Eve, and a few of the others that he cooked and served to their families came back whole. They became his wives and spent eternity having high-quality sex in their travels, their mansion sprawling in the middle of paradise.

The crazy old guy killing cats lost his urge to harm them and instead they became his favorite pets. He lived in the house on the top of the hill just to the side of heaven's gates. The guy hung out with Saint Peter and helped him recognize psychopaths. He became the steward of the biggest animal shelter in the celestial kingdom.

Joana, with her perfect feet, got the crown and prince. The female version of Jesus got a digestion system that turned piss and shit into wine and chocolate and she married the male version of the savior.

Kayla, Anaya, and all the other single ladies married rich, handsome, and stupid husbands who gave them a lot of money and were blind to their affairs. The girls spent their days on endless shopping tours, gossiping, and fucking with their gardeners, drivers, and security guards, while their husbands worked to provide for them.

While he was writing those last lines, Johnny wondered, were those husbands happy? And if not, how could he create a heaven for everyone if one's joy is based on injustice to others? Should he make Kayla, Anaya, and the other whores moral? he wondered. Johnny felt cold in his gut just at the thought. If all butterflies were to stick to one flower, the beauty of the meadow would die for good. He rejected the idea of heaven without whores. Therefore, he made their husbands unfaithful as well. Small fights and headaches over insignificant affairs make rich marriages truly sweet, he concluded.

Then came Indra's and Dominic's turn. Johnny called Lara to ask for advice but she repeated, "I don't know what could be salvation for a woman who keeps reincarnating for millennia only for her soulmate to kill her. Let alone for the man who was killing her. Maybe amnesia?"

Johnny liked the idea. He always had thought of oblivion as the place where true happiness lives. Should he erase the memory of not only Dominic and Indra but all his characters? Rage and suffering are the tormented souls' biggest enemies. Most of his creations were angry and devastated with sadness. Many of them dreamed of vengeance. Even if he gave them the ability to forgive others and themselves, and let go of their pasts, he knew they would remain crippled.

Deep down, he too felt crippled. When suffering lasts too long, the ability for happiness disappears, as if you have holes in your lungs. One can inhale but can never take a full breath. And all that could disappear with oblivion. But if he did that, the writer knew they would stop being who they were. Yet lucky people don't care about the past. Lucky people don't seek reasons and causes. They live in the present moment and go with the flow.

Eventually, Johnny discarded the idea of an eternal, pleasant oblivion. He wanted to heal their wounds and turn their scars into the foundations for the most beautiful love story in the entire history of the universe. He considered making them gods but they were too fragile for omnipotence and creation.

Dominic's words echoed in his thoughts, "Choices can be curses." Especially when you can choose whatever you want. At one point, he gave them a lot of cute kids and let them run a kindergarten. The writer decided that he believed children's laughter to be the best remedy for broken souls. Then he discarded that idea as well. He allowed Indra and Dominic to relive all their lives without the old vampire having to murder her. Both of them reincarnated with memories of previous lives and lived happily ever after with all their kids and families.

Johnny left the story that touched him the most for the end. Jenny did go to Harvard but failed to become the valedictorian. Her achievement was to be much greater. From the biggest cloud, with angels serving them food and drink, Ron and Oliver watched Jenny get a degree and prize for being the best student in the history of Harvard.

As for Ron and Oliver, they were free from beating and killing people for good. The writer even put all their victims to live on the same street as them. Oliver got a loan from the bank and bought an ice cream truck and Ron became a successful life coach. His popularity as a motivational speaker increased rapidly. The two of them married and adopted four orphans who had starved to death and moved to paradise without anyone.

Every character Johnny had ever created got his desire fulfilled in heaven. But when he finished the book, Johnny wasn't enthusiastic about it.

"It's insane," Lara assured him. "I've read nothing similar."

"I know, but something is missing," Johnny replied every time.

Then one day, he got an idea. His paradise lacked two people – the creator and his love. So, Johnny put himself and Lara inside. They lived in a beautiful cottage on the grassy shore on the edge of a river flowing from a lake with a great waterfall on the opposite side. Forest surrounded them. As for the chores, a maid came twice a week to set everything straight. A driver was always standing by, ready to take them to the best restaurants and nightclubs. Needless to say, Johnny made sure they were as rich as hell. Lara also had constant supervision over her two children who were still alive on Earth, who, of course, were doing well and getting richer every day.

"You won't believe this, but I have imagined us living this way," Lara said after reading it. "And, by the by, the book is now as complete as it can be."

"I will send it to the publishers tonight," Johnny said.

"What genre is it? A parody?"

"A satire, I would say," Johnny replied.

"I wish you luck," Lara said. "I have to go now. Keep in touch."

"Keep in touch."

That night, Johnny sent his manuscript to all the publishers he knew. It was two days after the New Year. Snow covered everything and it was as cold as the North Pole in the trailer. Lara had given Johnny money to rent an apartment, but he had spent it all on whores.

"You are crazy," she had told him. "I never understood why you don't find regular girls to fuck."

"I like beautiful girls. Besides you, no classy lady with pedicures, manicures, and soft skin would fuck with a poor shit like myself," he said.

Lara sighed. "You've told me that a thousand times."

"We never bore with repetitions."

Days passed with no replies. Only in the early spring did publishers send feedback. Two hundred refusals. "Two hundred fucking refusals," he hissed, hitting his head on the trailer wall. But then, after a couple of silent days spent flirting with suicide, mail came.

His name was Seymour. He was a famous midget who wrote scripts and directed movies. Three years ago, "Don't Save Dave" had earned eighty million at the box office in the first four weeks. Johnny was thrilled. His mother just kept repeating over the phone, "Didn't I tell you this day will come?"

A meeting was set for Friday. For two days, Johnny barely slept. He was too excited.

Seymour's office was on the last floor of the "Do-Do Movies" building, the glass tower with a sharp top piercing the clouds. It took a full minute for the fast elevator to climb to his office. When Johnny entered, it took all of his willpower not to burst out laughing. Seymour looked like a little doll made of crinkled wood. His chin hardly topped the edge of the enormous oak desk. His eyes blinked like malfunctioning streetlights.

A moment later, the writer realized the midget might be trying to stretch. His short arms were struggling to reach a fat cigar lying on the middle of the desk.

A tall guy in a black coat stood to his side. His skin was as tattooed dark as night and he was still as a statue. On the midget's other side was a fat white teenager with a hood over his head. His body swayed while his sharp gaze pierced Johnny's.

"Good evening?" Johnny said, taking a few shy steps forward.

"Good evening," Seymour replied, his eyes focused on the cigar.

Finally his tiny hands clutched it and brought it toward his mouth. But as his fingers trembled, the cigar fell on the table, and it rolled even farther away.

"Fucking assholes," he hissed and once more put his short arms to work. But the cigar was too far. Way beyond his reach. He struggled for some time. His strained face with a shit-like birthmark on the middle of his forehead contorted. The midget's eyes blinked while his hands tried to reach out just one more inch.

Johnny moved forward to help, but the tall tattooed guy waved his head and frowned. The writer interpreted it as a "Don't help him" and remained still. Seeing this the midget stopped. He leaned back on his big leather chair and his chin disappeared under the edge of the desk.

"Writer? I am glad you are here," he said. "Please, sit…"

"Thank you," the writer sat on the tiny chair in front of the desk.

"I must say, I don't see scripts like this very often," Seymour said.

"To be honest, I wrote it first as a book manuscript. But I wanted to try my luck everywhere."

"Luck? What is luck?"

"I think the answer depends on who you are," Johnny replied.

The teenager piped up about how he was tired and didn't see the point of his presence at the meeting. Seymour screamed at him about how he was old enough to know better than to interrupt them in the middle of an important conversation. Then he preached the boy about how he wanted him to see how the story business works. After emphasizing that many of his peers would kill to be in his shoes, Seymour threw the teenager out. James, as the big guy was called, silently went after Max, who slammed the door so hard they could hear the wall crack.

For the next half an hour, Seymour complained about how he did not know what to do with this nephew, his long-deceased brother's son. They had caught Max with weed more than once. And only two months ago, the kid had brought a loaded gun to school. If Seymour didn't have money for good lawyers, Max would have ended up in juvenile detention or even jail a long time ago.

Then Seymour switched back to the business at hand. "I have read Heavens for Everyone twice. I love it."

"Thank you."

"I like Dominic. Firm and aloof, even in heaven. And the narrative is unusual. It begins with the happy endings but still makes you fear and cheer for the characters, for all the characters, actually. Everyone is good. Everyone is a protagonist in some way. And the primary antagonist is life. It's everyone versus life and it's beautiful and unusual," Seymour was explaining.

A smile was spreading on Johnny's face.

"But let me tell you right now, 'Heavens for Everyone' will not be enough. It is far from enough. And I didn't love it because of what it is but because of what I believe it could be." The dwarf made a brief pause.

The silence felt hard in Johnny's ears.

"What I want to know," Seymour continued, "is how 'Heavens for Everyone' came to be? What triggered you to create something like that?"

"That is a very long story," Johnny sighed.

"We have time," Seymour retorted.

After thinking about it for a few moments, Johnny took a leap of faith and told the full truth. He told him everything about the night when the characters from his book appeared to prevent him from committing suicide. It was past midnight when the writer finished telling the midget the story.

"Splendid," Seymour was repeating. "A movie about writing a book to make a movie. Writers Inferno: Heaven for Everyone. I can see the beginning. Black screen with white letters: While there is madness, there is hope. The letters disappear and the blackness lessens slightly—just enough for the night to show how your trailer appears above the bridge railing. Then we buzz downstairs, cross the dark road with the broken streetlights, and enter your home when you pull the gun and put it in your mouth. No! We start with the gun in the mouth right away! Fuck! We will figure it out."

"I love it," Johnny said.

"Me too. I want to hit big with this movie. I want to win Oscars," Seymour said. "And you are going to help me. You will be with me at all times. And… Hell, after I heard all that, it's no wonder I have chosen you."

Both of them grew silent. Their eyes met. The midget was the one to speak first. "You see, the two of us are much alike. We are like brothers. We are so similar…"

"It doesn't seem like that," Johnny blurted with a smile.

The moment the word left his mouth, the writer felt grave regret, and he froze. The midget looked angry. His frowning brows fell to his mouth. Seymour was looking straight into Johnny's eyes. The midget's body rose as his little arms slid over the desk once more. The oak squeaked from the skin sliding over it. His tiny fingers almost reached the cigar. Yet, once again, he couldn't overpower that last remaining inch. Seymour gave up. He leaned back in his chair and started laughing. Johnny joined him.

"It doesn't look like that," he finally spoke. "But we are... We are both short. And let me tell you something... giants suffer much more than little ones when they can't reach the stars."

"And the most tormenting failures are when the achievements are only inches away," Johnny added.

"If you were someone else, I would throw you out right away. But short guys like us can joke among ourselves," he said. "Would you please hand me the cigar?"

"Sure."

"Thank you," Seymour said before his mouth embraced it.

He pulled a lighter from his pocket and lighted the cigar. Smoke rose from the red top and spread around the office.

"In one of your lines, you said that smoke fills you with hope. Because it starts chaotic but still rises. What do you hope for? Is it only for money and more pussy? Or is there something more?" Seymour asked.

"I love to write. I want to be free to create."

"I get it. You are free but the poverty is tiring. You don't have to worry about that anymore. I have prepared a contract for you. From this day forth, everything changes for you," Seymour said, pushing a piece of paper toward him.

Johnny could barely read it, he was so excited.

"I know how you feel," Seymour said. "I felt the same when I signed my first big contract. Will we go to a restaurant to celebrate?"

Suddenly, Johnny stopped reading. His gaze jumped from the paper to Seymour, his mouth open in amazement. "Here it says…"

"Yes," Seymour interrupted him. "You will get a part of the movie profits. We are partners, so to say."

Johnny signed both papers with trembling hands. Seymour took one. The midget's phone rang. When he answered it, a warm smile crept onto his face.

"I will come right away," he said and hung up. "I hope you will forgive me, but we will have to postpone our celebration." He paused briefly. "What can I say…? Mia does wonders… You will understand."

"Of course," Johnny replied.

They left the building together and parted ways at the first intersection.

10

The contract Johnny signed hadn't brought him a cent. Instead, it had made him Seymour's partner. When the time came, he would be sure to get his fair share of the profit. It meant that he would become a millionaire, a multi-millionaire. However, at the moment, his pockets remained empty. Seymour called it creative motivation. He did tip him with a few thousand bucks to relax: pay a visit to a whore, grab a lunch with his friends, and sniff a line or two. But not more than that.

"I want to keep your imagination running and give you just enough pleasure to invoke yearning. Suffering is a fuel for creation. I suffer because of what I am… And you suffer because you are poor. I will remain what I am for good, no matter what I do. But when money arrives, you might lose your fuel. When we cure your poverty, we could kill your art. And I need your art throughout the making of this movie," Seymour explained.

…

Three weeks passed since Johnny signed the contract. He used that time to write the first part of the script—Writer's Inferno. He agreed with Seymour, it was going to be the first part of the movie, preceding Heavens for Everyone. Johnny completed it in only a few days. Seymour loved it.

"Both your plot and dialogs as well as descriptions are very filmable," he said. "However, you go too far sometimes. Your imagination is wild. It needs to be tamed. No. Not tamed. It needs to be restrained... in some places... There is a character you need to change," Seymour told him.

Both of them burst out laughing. They remembered Ron and Oliver talking about hating changes.

"Which one?" Johnny asked.

"The warden," Seymour said and took a sip of whiskey before explaining. "It's a minor thing but it has to be done. The point of my story is: if everyone is insane, insane becomes normal. Normal becomes boring. For madness to endure and remain what it is, you need to have a hook of normality. A dot of opposition that will stand out as a black blur on a clean white sheet. Someone who will make all those crazy lads look even crazier."

"The warden needs to become normal?" Johnny asked.

"Yes," Seymour said. "Presented within such a small space, his cannibalism doesn't look convincing enough. It's more like someone crammed bizarre mental illnesses and deviations into one sack and then turned it into a person just to fit it in the story."

"I think it will thrill him to find out he isn't eating his wives anymore," Johnny added.

They chuckled. The bartender brought two medium-rare steaks to their table. Cutting the meat with a sharp knife, Seymour exclaimed, "Fuck it! I am falling in love."

"Yes, the steak is wonderful," Johnny said.

"I'm not talking about the meat. I feel guilty for eating it. That means I am falling in love with Mia," the midget said. "She flips out when I eat meat, screams about how cruel I am. When we are together, it's only plants… I promised her I would eat less meat…" After a brief pause, he continued with a wondering gaze, "I never understood vegans. Plants are alive too. But not every blood is red."

"Neither does every wound bleed," Johnny said. "I get you. Vegans are like the killers of plants. And we who eat everything are only participants in the food chain. Vegans decide which beings are worthy of life and which are not. And they consider plants edible only because they don't move and are still and silent."

Johnny stabbed a piece of steak with his fork, lifted it to his mouth, and swallowed it.

"My point. It's okay to kill and eat plants. Unless you are a company cutting down the rainforest. Then it's wrong because we remember that plants give us air."

"Did you ever say that to Mia?"

"I don't do philosophy with women."

Johnny chuckled. "An excellent decision. While we are speaking of food, maybe the warden could become a vegan," the writer said.

Seymour stopped to think about it, "Maybe…"

He told Johnny he should also reduce the time spent with the snake in the trunk and say a word or two about the title "Song for a Grave."

…

That night, Johnny started the warden's remake. He turned him into an ordinary man whose wife, Eve, was a vegan. They had small fights over the orders in the restaurant and that was pretty much it about good old George.

He shortened the chapter with the snake and trunk.

As for the "Song for a Grave," Johnny wrote a few more lines about Madelyn. She dedicated her song to her fallen brother and her husband. They had disappeared in the war. Both of them were pilots who flew together over the ocean before they vanished. Madelyn never stopped believing they were still alive on some faraway island, waiting for a ship to sail along and save them. Before singing, she would always say, "This is a song for two very special guests I am expecting tonight." She never married or had any other man but the one she was waiting for.

…

Seymour was pleased. It was time to start the casting.

"I want new actors. New faces for a new movie," Seymour said. "I want this to be a magnificent piece of art."

And the search started. They left the actor who would play the writer for the very end. "We are more defined by what we are not than what we are. Our borderlines give us shape. And others draw the borders," the midget explained. "We must shape those borders into a masterpiece. That is why we start with the main side characters. All those characters, names, and titles exist for one purpose only—to express the protagonist. The greater they are, the more magnificent the protagonist will be. We must choose wisely and establish high standards."

Johnny could not agree more. The first audition was for Indra.

"A woman is a man's reflection. But rarely does she reflect what a man has. Much more often, she carries what her man lacks from the inside," he said.

"Hope," Johnny murmured.

"Exactly," Seymour agreed.

He insisted Johnny take part in the casting. Seymour's nephew, Max, got a job as well. A golden plate with his name was standing in the middle of the table for the casting directors. The midget sat on the right, Johnny was on his left, while two professors from the drama academy, Paul and Jean, took the edges. The stage with the red curtains sprawled out in front of them in an empty theater on the outskirts of the town. Not only were the seats in the theater full, but girls stood in a long line outside too. Yet the actresses were disappointing, to say the least. Some couldn't even read the lines properly. Max loved them all.

"I think she was pretty good," he said for every single one, his face blushing.

One actress enchanted him most. She neared the table, her gaze fixed on Max's, and said, "You can have any woman in here. Even me. I love him with all my heart. I love him so much I would do anything to save him."

It looked like Max attempted to read the next line in the script. But he wasn't capable not only of reading–the poor guy couldn't even swallow. He wasn't blushing any more. His face turned red, like melting metal.

Seymour said, "My nephew is acting like a virgin boy who can't say anything to a pretty lady apart from, 'you are good!'"

The whole theater burst into laughter. Max threw his copy of the script and ran outside. Sheets flew all over the stage.

"Come back! I was just kidding! Max!" Seymour yelled, but mad Max didn't even turn. He slammed the door, making cracks in the surrounding walls. James ran after him.

"Virginity is not for mockery," Johnny whispered. "Teenagers are very sensitive about that."

"I am an idiot sometimes," the midget admitted as the casting continued.

. . .

For the next two days, the middle seat remained empty.

"I love him with all my heart! And I would do anything to save him," all the actresses were saying.

It didn't sound truthful, and at some point, Seymour got so agitated by their acting that he climbed on the table and started yelling.

"Ladies! Please! For God's sake! You are not in court trying to prove your innocence! In acting, you need to look guilty! Guilty of who you are. And you are a woman in love! What's your name again, sweetheart?" Seymour asked the woman standing in the middle of the stage.

"Jenny," she replied.

"All right, Jenny. For five thousand years, your soul mate has been killing you. He's ripped the heart from your chest. And you reincarnated only to experience that same story again. Now, as Indra, you remember all your previous lives and you still love him. More than ever! Despite him once killing all of your children," Seymour explained. "He slaughtered your children in the wheat field. It is love. But not any kind of love. Your love is primordial. That means it's not about making your face look the right way. Or your eyes to moist. Or your body to tremble. It is about dedicating the core of your existence to that love and allowing the consequences to manifest themselves."

Jenny's chin was quivering. "So, I don't get the role?"

"Get the role! You can barely roll your tongue!" Seymour roared.

She burst into tears and ran from the stage. Johnny wanted to go after her, but Seymour grabbed his wrist and said, "Leave her be… Mockery and refusals are the foundations of prosperity."

"She looked overly upset," one professor noticed.

"Way too upset," Johnny added. "She looked like she could…"

"She'll get over it," Seymour interrupted. "The girl will cry it out loud in her room. Pain will help her discover parts of her she didn't even know existed. And it will make her a better actress. Next!"

Johnny couldn't let it go. A chilly feeling in his gut gnawed at him. Like in the times of his strongest anxieties. He said he would return shortly and rushed after her. But when the writer went out, there was no trace of Jenny. He wandered around for quite a time. Then he pulled himself together and went back. When he entered the theater, Seymour was still on the loose, standing on the table and roaring. Another girl's chin was quivering. With her head down, she was leaving the stage.

"Next!"

The first actress worthy of the role appeared a couple of days later. She had big green eyes and a warm face framed by long black hair. Her figure was lush under a long yellow dress. After taking her place on the stage, not a word came out of her mouth. She was only standing and gazing at Seymour. Max drooled at the woman without even trying to be discrete or decent.

"Shall we begin?" Seymour asked.

"Our story began a long time ago... Don't you recognize me?" she retorted with a bold look in her eyes.

"Could you please hold on to the script? There will come a part for improvisation," Seymour said.

"I want you to change the script. You owe him that much!"

"I owe him nothing. Please, return to the script."

"What if I can make it better? The script? I can help you turn it into a fairy tale," she said, slowly approaching the table and lowering her head toward Seymour's. Gently looking at him, the actress asked, "What if I could help you seize what has been out of your reach for so long?"

"Hold on to the script. I will not repeat it twice," Seymour said.

"You could be tall and handsome!"

"The casting has rules!" Seymour hissed.

Max chuckled.

"Art is about breaking rules. Melting them into chaos. Then molding chaos to your desires. Did you ever feel the kiss of a pretty woman without having to pay her?" she asked, her lips close to Seymour's. He said nothing. It looked like the midget was surprised as well. She cupped his head and pushed her tongue into his mouth. At first, Seymour didn't move. But after a few moments, he kissed her back. Suddenly, she moved back. Although the kiss was over, the midget was still panting. She brought her lips to his ear and whispered something. Seymour blanched.

"I can do nothing else but hope you will change the script," she said, climbing down from the stage.

"Wait," Johnny called after her. "We want to see more."

She stopped, looked back over her shoulder, and said, "And that is exactly the point of every art. To make people wish for more."

Then she continued toward the exit.

"Come back. You are fantastic," Max yelled before she went through the door. "Is she going to come back?" The teenager was dumbstruck.

"I don't think so," Seymour mumbled.

"She really left? Gave up the role?" Max couldn't calm down.

"What was that all about?" Johnny asked.

"Fear of success. Some people just can't cope with it," Seymour replied. "Next!"

Johnny thought there was something strange about it. At the end of the day, he asked Seymour what she whispered to him.

"She murmured some stupid love chant that I couldn't fully understand," he replied.

Johnny thought Seymour was lying, but decided not to press it. It took them another few weeks to find their Indra. Three girls made it to the finals. The casting directors chose Alyssa. She dominated the improvisation part that Seymour deemed the most important.

"There is an old saying in the village I came from. When sheep are bleating, the grass hears howling. Who the wolf is depends on who you are. That is why I don't want to judge anyone. Or to hate. All I want is to love! Please," she was looking Johnny straight in the eye. "Please, give us a chance. At least one life." A tear ran down her face.

Seymour, Johnny, Max, and both of the professors loved it and decided that she was the one. It was evening when they officially closed the casting for Indra and went to celebrate. Max persuaded them to go to a shooting range. He wanted them to let out some steam. Johnny, Seymour, and James were sitting and drinking coffee, watching Max raging with the shotgun. The targets, some twenty yards away, burst into pieces. That didn't prevent Max from reloading and shooting. It wasn't about hitting the target but about releasing an explosion. And there was love in the way he held that gun. Loaded it with bullets. Pulled the trigger.

"I have adopted a mad Max," Seymour said.

Johnny and James chuckled.

"But under all that attitude and guns is only a scared little child who lost both parents too early," Seymour added.

"Did he ever have a woman?" Johnny asked.

"No. You saw how he reacted. When I try to talk to him about it, he pushes me away. Won't even allow me to broach the subject. That is what I wanted to ask you all this time. Could you take care of it? Naturally, I will give you money for all the expenses," Seymour asked.

"Of course," Johnny replied.

"I think women might pull him away from those weapons," Seymour said.

"I wouldn't agree," James piped up. "I am sorry to break it to you, but weapons are a passion. It is about holding the power of death in your hands."

"I was hoping I could tempt him to hold a pen. That also gives you power over death. And life. With a pen you become God," Seymour said.

"Maybe to your characters. But when you hold a shotgun, you become God to anyone," James retorted. "A real God!"

"I can hope pussy will change him," Seymour said.

"Pussy is a powerful weapon," Johnny agreed. "I guess we can wait and see."

11

After the first day of casting for Dominic, Johnny suggested to Max to go for a drink together.

"Don't you corrupt him," Seymour butted in. "He is still underage."

"I am turning eighteen next week," Max protested.

"Until then, you will live like a seventeen-year-old," Seymour retorted. "And you can't go."

"You are not my father! I will do whatever I want!" Max shouted.

"That is true. Well, then... Do whatever you want, but this time, there is no avoiding jail. I will not bust my ass to pay all those lawyers to clean up after you!" Seymour concluded firmly before leaving the theater.

...

Not in his craziest dreams could Max guess that this was all part of the plan. Nelly was already sitting in the bar's corner and waiting for them. They had paid her in advance for an entire night of GFE, girlfriend experience—kissing, cuddling, and everything else needed for the event to feel real. Max had a thing for short brunettes with big tits. She easily dragged him away from Johnny and left the writer sitting alone at the bar.

He didn't remain alone with his thoughts for long. A brunette in a short fluttery dress and black open-toe high heels approached him, her feet as gentle as silk, with petal-like nails painted red.

"Are you bored?" she asked, taking a seat next to him.

"Not anymore," he replied.

"Could you please look at this?" the girl asked politely, pushing her phone in front of his face.

A video of a fight was playing. A stout, short, black-haired woman was beating the shit out of the pretty girl – dragging and throwing her around as if she was a toy. The fight was taking place on the street. The pretty girl was wearing light blue jeans, and she was barefoot. She fell into a muddy puddle. Her wet soles shined under the light of phone cameras while the woman punched her in the head. The pretty girl was groaning like she was being fucked. A man came between the two of them and stopped the fight.

"I pissed myself. Luckily, there was a puddle I could blame for being wet," she said.

Johnny's cock was as hard as stone.

"You should not fight," he said. "You are too pretty to risk scars."

"Thank you… I am here for the audition," she replied. "I want Kayla's role."

Johnny stopped for a moment to think. "The castings for the side female characters will start once we find Dominic," he finally replied. "You will get your chance then…"

"I think this is the perfect place for casting," she interrupted him. "You see, last week I fucked that woman's husband. He gave me his entire salary to buy something nice. But he also took photos of me in their bed. I followed you to this bar. Before I approached you, I sent her the photos of me with her husband. And of these Gucci pumps that I bought."

She opened WhatsApp to show him. After a series of photos ending with one of her feet, there was a message, "Your husband bought me these beautiful shoes. I put them on and went for a walk. I know he doesn't earn much and gave me the last penny for them. So, if you don't have any money, you can come here. I will buy you a coffee…"

There was no answer, but the wife saw the message.

"Do you think that she will come?"

"She will come… Any moment now," she said.

"You shouldn't do it…" Johnny started.

"Oh, come on! Stop pretending. I read the script. You love watching women tearing each other apart. Sorry," she corrected herself right away, "My bad… You like to watch one-sided catfights in which the pretty girl is beaten and humiliated…"

Although he tried to keep it serious, Johnny's face split into a twisted smile. His cock was attempting to pierce the jeans. That little stream of sperm that gets you alimony before you even cum was wetting his boxers. Her legs were crossed and her upper foot was within reach of his hand.

"I could use a foot massage," she said with a raunchy look in her eyes.

He gently slid his fingers under the shoe and onto her foot. The sole was as gentle as a pillow in a silk pillowcase. And a little wet. Johnny never minded sweat on beautiful women.

"I cannot guarantee you the role," Johnny said. "It's not up to me."

"Nothing in life is guaranteed," she replied and looked toward the entrance. "She is coming."

The writer turned. A short brunette, ugly and fat, strode into the bar. She wasn't wearing any shoes and her feet resembled bricks. The actress tried to defend herself, but the brunette just shoved her hands in her hair and forced her down. All the guests froze, gaping at the two ladies. Johnny stood up right away, but did it slow enough to satisfy his urges at least a bit. The actress groaned a few times when the woman's strong palm slapped her. Her shoes flew off her feet and her legs flew up and spread. A beautiful, shaved pussy flashed.

Johnny jumped between them. The bartender joined him and a couple of the male guests rushed to the actress' aid. Even the police came. They took Anna, the ugly brunette, with them. The actress, who identified herself as Cristin, didn't want to press any charges or come with them.

"I want to go home," she said, tears running down her stained face. A thin, bloody rivulet trickled from her nose and there was a barely visible bruise under her left eye.

When the police left with Anna, Cristin and Johnny went to his trailer. Her mere presence was pushing him to the brink of cuming. She was very flexible. Her sweaty soles ended on his face, sliding over his opened mouth with his tongue sticking out. He entered her tiny wet hole. Slowly, he moved his hips forward and backward until he filled the condom with his progeny. When he got out, Cristin turned and put her feet on his chest.

"If it was up to you, would I pass the audition?"

"You were born to be Kayla," he said.

They fucked more. After that, Johnny said he needed to sleep and offered to call her a cab. When a vehicle arrived, she kissed him and went out barefoot.

"Your shoes?" Johnny called after her.

"Keep them as souvenirs," she said and left.

...

Johnny fell asleep. The phone ringing woke him a little after dawn. It was Seymour.

"Jenny killed herself!" he shouted.

"Who?" Johnny was confused.

"Jenny! That girl who cried and rushed out of the theater during the audition for Indra," he said.

"Fuck?"

"Did I do it?"

"What? No!"

"Tell me honestly! Did I kill her?" Seymour went on.

"No! You were harsh. That is true! But you didn't kill her. What she did was her choice and her choice only," Johnny assured him.

"Poor girl. She jumped from the twentieth floor. Most people die of a heart attack before they touch the concrete. But not her. She smashed and stayed alive. Choked on the blood in her lungs pierced by her broken ribs," he said. They were both silent for a couple of moments. "Can you imagine such a disappointment that stripped her of fear and made her drown in her own bloodstream?"

"Yes, I can... I was close to that once... It's not your fault," Johnny repeated.

...

The casting was closed for the day. The national television reported about the suicide. There was good news too: Max wasn't a virgin anymore. Nelly texted Johnny that the boy even had the potential to be a great lover. But the writer was going to leave that discussion for some other time.

The next day, the newspapers were full of Seymour's photographs. Most titles were accusing him of the tragedy and suggesting that the filming should stop. Seymour was well-known for his cruelty towards young actors. He even had a few lawsuits going on since several actors had pressed charges about his abuses. But that didn't stop those who wanted Dominic's role to fill the theater and eagerly wait for their turn to audition.

"It feels good to be final. From the perspective of tormenting immortality, the ability to die is a great power. I guess death is the deity of immortality," they were each saying.

Then, they would continue with, "Good evening. Forgive me for not standing up. But considering the circumstances, I believe my manners are not of great importance."

As Seymour explained, the point was to see the actor's ability to switch from sadness to cynicism and then to rage. There was a line of threats Dominic was supposed to say to frighten them. The actors seemed disappointing even to Johnny, who knew nothing about acting.

Max didn't hide his disappointment. "You should start your YouTube channel. Call it, how to fail in life," he shouted at one. "Are you just acting that you want to act in this movie?"

But Seymour was firm in his decision to star fresh faces. The mockery continued until a tall, pale man stepped on the stage. He had a rough accent. Probably Russian. When he started speaking, Johnny thought for a moment that Dominic returned.

He didn't start with the provided lines, but with threats. The actor was looking at Seymour disdainfully while words as cold as Siberia flew from his mouth. "I thought of cutting off your head and stretching your spine until your corpse becomes long enough for a regular casket. But then I remembered corpses don't suffer. And dead men pay no debts. That is why I decided Max here is the best choice. The clock is ticking."

While he spoke, it looked like the words were turning into a mortar that glued itself to Seymour's face. When the guy finished, the midget was pale as a frozen corpse. Without a word, the man walked from the stage.

"Wait!" Max shouted. "We want to hear more."

But the man didn't respond, he just continued towards the exit.

"Don't you want the part?" Johnny called after him and turned toward Seymour. "He is incredible. Right? Why is he going away?"

"Fear of success," the midget said after a few silent moments. "Next!"

Johnny said nothing. But he didn't believe him. There was something more to it. There was something more to it now and that time the woman kissed the midget and whispered something in his ear. Seymour was absent for the rest of the day. He looked through the actors and spoke mechanically about acting, but the color didn't return to his face.

When the casting ended for the day, Johnny asked Seymour about the pale guy again, but got the same reply. Then Johnny mentioned Cristin and told Seymour what happened.

"Are you insane!?" Seymour flipped out. "She will press charges. All the people in the bar witnessed that you left together. I bet she has cab drivers to confirm that she went to and from your place."

Johnny dropped his head. "Fuck! You are right."

"It's my fault. I should have warned you about it… It is a typical scam," Seymour said. "What's done is done. The future will tell."

And indeed, it wasn't long before Seymour's grim predictions became reality. Cristin's lawyer called Seymour to inform him that they will press charges against Johnny unless her client gets an appropriate compensation. The midget said he would think about it.

"We must be realistic. If Jenny didn't kill herself, we could go to court. But with Jenny's death and all the other stuff going on, it would be us fighting on too many fronts," Seymour explained.

"Other stuff?" Johnny asked in surprise.

"I have some private issues," the midget said as his gaze danced around. "Long story. Anyway, Cristin will do great as Kayla. She really is born for that part."

…

It took them three weeks to find Dominic. The guy wasn't as tall and pale but, as Seymour said, "In movie-making, angles turn hugs into strangles. If used the right way, a camera can turn dwarfs into giants, let alone an average-sized dark guy to a tall and pale one."

His name was Justin. He wasn't as good as the strange Russian guy, but he carried that same cold energy, and his gaze and voice were as sharp as knives.

"Shame for that Russian guy," Johnny muttered.

"Justin will do great," Seymour retorted. "Don't doubt me for a moment. I would rather not make a movie than make a lousy one! Understand?"

"Yes. Justin will do great," Johnny said.

Lara was next. After only two days, Johnny called his muse to ask if she has a long-lost twin sister.

"I mean, the actress we discovered today is literally your double," he repeated.

"I can't wait to see the movie. I am so happy for you," Lara gushed.

"You will live like a queen," Johnny said.

"I hope so… I am so tired of everything," she said and started in a long tirade about Edin torturing her again.

Her ex-husband had ended up in jail and Simon, the rich Greek giving her money, had reduced her allowance. Lara wouldn't stop talking. At some point, Johnny had to interrupt her since he had to go to the audition but promised to call her as soon as he could squeeze in a few spare minutes.

. . .

Now they had to choose Oliver, Ron, and other side characters. It was much easier to find them. Ron had over six candidates who would all do great. Over ten actors seemed suitable for Oliver's part.

At some point, an attractive brunette entered the theater. It looked like nature wanted her face to depict ancient perversions. She had a beautiful body with skin that looked soft and gentle, like silk.

"Let's take a break!" Seymour exclaimed.

Before he stood up, she had already leaned in front of the table and planted her lips on Seymour's. The kiss exploded. Everyone was pretending nothing was going on but all the faces and eyes carried a hint of a mocking smile. Except for Max. He started singing, "Seymour has a girlfriend! Seymour has a girlfriend!"

"Shut the fuck up!" the midget yelled.

"Why should he? He is not lying," Mia said.

"No. He is not," Seymour agreed. His voice was low, and he looked sideways. "What brings you here?"

"Are you ashamed of me?" she asked.

"Ashamed. No. Why?"

"I wanted to stop by and see how you're doing... I thought you could use a break and the two of us could grab a lunch," she said.

"Sure. Why not?" Seymour agreed.

He slid from the chair, almost falling. Mia took his hand, and they went out. While they were leaving, it looked like she was taking a child for a walk.

"We will continue in an hour!" Seymour said before they went through the door.

...

After an hour, Seymour called Johnny to say the casting would continue tomorrow. The actors left quickly. Johnny, James, and Max went to grab something to eat.

"She will destroy him," Max said.

"Why do you think that?"

"Oh, come on!" Max yelped at the writer. "My uncle is a midget. And she is a hot pussy. Those things don't match up. Even I know that much."

James' face split into a smile. They were quiet for some time. Then Max insisted they proceed to the shooting range. Both Johnny and James thought it was a bad idea. But Max just wouldn't stop. "I need some practice. After all, Uncle promised to put me in charge of the armory when we start filming," Max said.

"Really?" Johnny asked in disbelief.

"He was there," Max said, pointing at James.

"I was there," James confirmed.

On the way to the shooting range, Max couldn't stop smiling. He was getting dozens of messages from Nelly but didn't reply.

"I have my priorities," he said.

Max took a shotgun and fired for almost an entire hour. He opened the gun and loaded it with bullets as if it was a toy. More than once, the barrel swung toward other people. Luckily, Johnny and James were the only ones to notice. James approached him to mention something about it, but Max just said, "Relax! I know what I am doing."

…

The next day, the casting continued. All went smoothly. It was much easier to choose the side characters. Seymour said the hardest part was yet to come. Finding the writer.

12

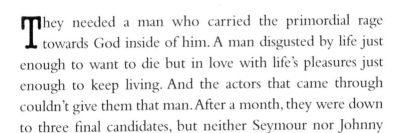

They needed a man who carried the primordial rage towards God inside of him. A man disgusted by life just enough to want to die but in love with life's pleasures just enough to keep living. And the actors that came through couldn't give them that man. After a month, they were down to three final candidates, but neither Seymour nor Johnny nor the two professors were thrilled with them.

"Emanuel," Seymour was shouting as another long day at the theater was ending. "You are one finalist. Can't you, for the love of God, show some actual rage?"

Emanuel raised his head as if to pierce the ceiling with his eyes and shouted, "It was enough! You will torture me no more!"

"It's not enough! You need to draw rage from the depths of your soul. Can't you be angrier because he makes you wash dishes all day long just to pay the rent? That he made you bury your parents before you were ten and grow up in orphanages while some of your peers fucked pretty girls and enjoyed themselves in pools in the backyards of their mansions?"

"You will torment me no more!" Emanuel screamed.

"Better... All right, enough for today," Seymour said.

"It isn't about their acting. It is more about the fact that you can't train a rookie to become a war veteran. You can teach him to shoot, but he needs to survive the battles," the midget explained when they were alone in the theater.

The professor didn't stop trying to persuade him to hire someone famous. "This role requires an actor with a lot of experience. And you can have anyone you want. I don't know an actor who would refuse a part in your movie."

"No," Seymour protested sharply. "When you give a role to a Brad Pitt, it becomes a Brad Pitt movie. What I want to make must not be associated with any famous name."

Johnny opened his mouth to say something, but Seymour's phone rang.

"Is he all right? I am on my way!" Seymour jumped from the chair and raced towards the exit. Johnny followed. They rushed into the Limo.

"Quickly! To the city hospital!" Seymour shouted.

His driver, Chen, stepped on the gas.

"What happened?" Johnny asked.

Seymour didn't answer. He was panting. He took a bottle of whiskey from the mini-bar, removed the lid, and brought the bottle to his mouth. The liquid ran into his throat like a river.

"What happened?" Johnny repeated.

"Max got shot at the shooting range!"

"Is he all right?"

"I don't know. Oh my God, it's all my fault!"

"Calm down!"

"It's my fault! Oh, my God! It's all my fault!" Seymour repeated.

It looked as if he had lost the ability to say anything else. He was on the brink of tears. The same words kept escaping his mouth as he rushed through the hospital toward Max's room. Seymour didn't hear the nurse say his nephew was fine since the bullet only brushed the flesh on his thigh. He strode into the room as if running to hear his last words. Max was sitting on the bed with an ice cream in one hand and his phone in the other.

"Oh my God, you are fine," Seymour sighed deeply.

"Yes, I am fine," Max replied, tapping his phone. He didn't even look up from the screen. "Some drunk idiot lost his balance and shot me in the thigh."

"I saw that the guy was risky right away," James piped in. "I told the security guy they shouldn't let him shoot, but they said they can't throw the man out just for looking unreliable."

"And the fool just couldn't stop talking to me," Max added. "I feel as if I'm a magnet for idiots."

"What was he saying?" Seymour asked, but Max didn't answer. He just kept tapping his phone. "What was he say-ing?" Seymour yelled.

"What's wrong with you? Why are you yelling at me? I don't remember. He was talking about banks and debts. Leave me alone. I am texting with Nelly," Max blurted out.

"Now he has two passions. Guns and ladies," Johnny said with a raunchy gaze. "And what happened to the guy who shot you? Did the police take him away?"

"They are still looking for him. He ran from the shooting range as soon as the gun fired," James answered instead of Max.

A nurse came in to tell them that visiting hours were over. Max was supposed to stay in the hospital for only a couple of days while the stitches on his thigh heals. Seymour instructed James to stay in front of the building all night and monitor who goes in and out. James nodded and went out to his car in the parking lot.

"This shooting was not an accident," Seymour added. "It was a warning. I didn't think they would go this far…"

"A warning?" Johnny was confused.

Seymour didn't want to explain further, but he invited Johnny to drop by at his penthouse. He wanted to talk about the future of the movie.

"There are some things you don't know," he said during the ride. "But we will discuss them when we are alone."

When they arrived at the penthouse, Johnny found out that Seymour had unsettled matters with some mean and dangerous loan sharks from Hollywood. They were the ones who had sent those two odd actors to threaten him on the stage.

"That Dominic guy? And the girl pretending to be Indra…?"

"Gang members," Seymour interrupted him. "That is why they were the best. No actor can out act the truth."

"Why are they doing this?" Johnny asked.

"A long time ago, when I was raising funds for my first movie, I was penniless," Seymour began.

"The Sixth Life of a Black Cat?" Johnny asked.

"Yes… The Sixth Life of a Black Cat," Seymour confirmed. "There is no need to tell you how desperate I was. You know better than anyone how much an artist suffers when they can't create. Especially when they can't do it because of poverty. I didn't even have enough to pay my part of the rent. No one would employ me. I went along as a magician at children's birthday parties. Being a doll to six- and seven-year-olds who are taller than you. Sucks, right?"

"I can't say it doesn't," Johnny agreed.

"So I quit. I said to myself, either I will find people to fund my movie and go up, or I will find a bridge and go down," Seymour made a brief pause. He was rolling a glass of whiskey between his fingers, absently gazing into space. "So, there I was in a little room with two beds and without money to pay the rent. At some point, my roommate felt sorry for me and told me he might have a way for me to get cash. His ex was an actress struggling to make a living acting and knew some shady guys from Hollywood. Loan sharks. Dangerous loan sharks. They gave me cash to fund my movie. And I gave them half of my earnings. It was fair. But that wasn't enough. They kept asking for money every time I released a new movie. Money and movie rights. I gave them half of my money after the second and third movie, but then I said it was enough.

I teamed up with a few scriptwriters and actors, and we went to the police to press charges. It was a hard fight. They were rich and powerful, with a lot of inside people. But after two years, the police caught them and put them behind bars. A few of them had murders on their hands and even got life sentences. Some of them died. Some of them got killed in prison fights. I thought it was over for good. But then, only a few days after we met, when I announced the casting, I got that phone call." Seymour trailed off. He took a sip of whiskey, absently looking through the windows of his penthouse. The city was shining like a rich man's whore. Before Johnny said anything, the little man continued, "It was that quiet voice. It said: Good day, I found your name on the list. I knew who it was right away."

"Did you go to the police?" Johnny asked.

"I did. A friend of mine is a detective. I told him everything as soon as I got the call. But what could he do? I called him when the actors started coming. But you can't charge actors for acting, now can you?" Seymour replied.

"You can't. But this was shooting. They will catch him for sure," Johnny said.

"It's not enough. They need to prove the gang is involved. They will hardly be able to do that," Seymour explained.

"Didn't you know what you were getting into?" Johnny asked.

"It was a long time ago. I heard stories. But tell me, would there be a story scary enough to repel you from your desires?"

"I understand," the writer said after a brief pause. "To build foundations, you need to go underground and get dirty. And poor people must start from the foundations. We know that better than anyone. Those who have no rich cousins must seek help from the devil."

"God is deaf and blind for the suffering of the poor," Seymour added.

"How much do they want?" the writer asked.

"This time, it's not about money," Seymour replied.

"Then what is it about?"

"They want to take part in the moviemaking." Seymour made a brief pause. "They want me to make a thirty-second scene with a church in it."

"A church?"

"A Scientology fraction presented in a good way. I was told that we should add a Good Samaritan guy among your characters. The guy would give his life to save your's and, with his last breath, tell you to visit the church," Seymour explained.

"Will you do it?"

"I wanted to ask for your opinion." Seymour looked at him pointedly. "We are partners, after all…"

"It's a hard call," Johnny made a brief pause. "You know, just this morning, my mother called to see how the castings went. She is thrilled that my book is being adapted into a movie, to say the least... And proud..."

"She has reason to be proud. Her son is a very gifted man," Seymour said.

Johnny smiled. "There is one thing... She was advising me as to how we should choose the actor. She wanted to come on to the audition. I told her that it was out of the question."

"She can come whenever she pleases."

"My point is... How do I say this...? Yes... If you allow everyone to touch a sculpture, then everyone becomes the sculptor, and the masterpiece quickly turns into a miscreation," Johnny made a brief pause. "We really are much alike. I consider you to be a very smart man. And you know that money means more to me than anything else."

"I know."

"But if you allow people to get into your stuff too much... It won't be what you imagined it to be... It's your call," Johnny concluded.

"I love Max too much to let anything happen to him," Seymour said.

"A Good Samaritan from some crazy church is more than suitable for the movie," Johnny mused.

"You agree?" Seymour asked. "Because I will do nothing without you."

"Yes, I agree. Max's life is more important. Besides, the movie can only be better with that new freak," Johnny said.

"That settles it," Seymour concluded.

His phone rang. The midget's grim face split into a smile. Mia had sent him a message.

"Are you falling in love?" Johnny asked, barely refraining from bursting into laughter.

"No… But tell me… Is there a chance that a woman is really twisted enough to be attracted to…" Seymour asked.

"There is a chance for everything," Johnny said. "I knew a guy who was into women who lacked a leg. An amputee devotee, he called it."

Seymour burst out laughing. "It pleases me to hear such things."

"And it makes me think that in the heart of this harsh world, there is mercy and compassion, after all," Johnny said.

"Oh, really…?"

"Yes… Every man or woman with a cripple fetish is a gift to those who are malformed. If Mia is really as twisted as that, you can be God to her," Johnny said.

"That's what I've started to think. We have been seeing each other for a couple of months, and she takes no money from me. She is well-to-do herself. I think she enjoys the sex… We do it everywhere. She doesn't wear panties. She puts on a dress and just stands above me. I tilt my head back and start licking."

"That's nice," Johnny said, chuckling.

"We do it everywhere. In the toilet. In the elevator. We even did it on the street."

"On the street?"

"Yes. She wore a long dress that covered even her feet. And I slide in and start licking. She squirts every time. You can't fake squirting, can you?" Seymour's eyes shone with hope.

"You can't. There is no question about it," Johnny assured him.

"Maybe, just maybe, I think she might be the one. I don't want to raise my hopes too much."

"With women, hopes can easily turn into ropes and men will always be the ones left hanging," Johnny mused.

13

Johnny had never seen Seymour so agitated. His face was as red as flowing lava. The midget's little body was hopping and twitching while he yelled at the camera operator.

"You are what fits you. And if shit fits in your mouth, it means you are a toilet! And tonight, you are full of shit. You are saying a lot of shit. And doing a lot of shit! And I already have a toilet seat on the set. I don't need another one. Do you get that?"

The guy nodded silently.

"Then put the fucking cameras like I told you to… And don't tell me about the angles. I could turn a duck into a fuck on which you would jerk yourself to death… If I wanted to…," Seymour concluded.

After the guy finished his job, he rushed out of the trailer as fast as he could. The writer and Seymour remained alone. Johnny didn't dare ask what was wrong. However, while they were waiting for the actors to arrive, Seymour told him everything.

"It's Mia."

"What is it?"

"Well… She isn't into little men."

Seymour remained speechless for some time. Then he finally opened up, "It was vengeance. Because I didn't give her some stupid role ten years ago. I didn't recognize her. But her face looked familiar. Mia remembered everything. She wanted to mess with my head before my next filming. She would have never fucked with me for free… And she told me so last night. Right after she sucked me off. She also told me she wasn't squirting…"

"Oh…?" Johnny struggled not to laugh.

"That's right. Be free to laugh. She was pissing on me all that time. And squeezing the stream of her piss so it looked like squirting," he said.

Johnny was laughing hysterically.

"That's not all," Seymour continued. "Mia explained that she has some strange bacteria in her piss. She told me that this was another reason she forced herself to piss on my face, down my throat… So I would get sick… And this last month I have been feeling like my throat is all swollen…"

"How couldn't you tell it was urine?" Johnny asked.

"I've never tasted piss." Seymour looked at him significantly.

"Good point," Johnny said. "What did you do?"

"I threw her out…"

"That sucks," Johnny almost whispered.

"Yes… I didn't sleep at all. Strangely, I thought a lot about you after she left. And felt pain in my chest."

"About me?"

"I was wondering… If the quality of happiness doesn't exceed the quantity of suffering, why should we live?" Seymour asked, staring at his malformed reflection in the shiny colt standing on the edge of the table.

"I think you should stop thinking about that," Johnny remarked and put his hand on the midget's shoulder. "Reason is treason to happiness," he added.

"Then I am a treacherous man," Seymour said. "You know… I don't think I ever accepted being a dwarf…"

"I don't think any soul with dignity can accept being imprisoned in the dungeon of genetic garbage," Johnny replied. "But it doesn't matter what you are. It's how you feel, that's what is important…"

"I feel like shit," Seymour interrupted him.

"I'd rather be a happy shit than a sad star. And what is rich can always be happy."

"It's not about the money. I get bored with the whores. Then you start looking for something different. Some people call it love." Seymour looked Johnny in the eye. "But right now it looks like a midget like me can't be loved."

"There is no love… only lies. And a good lie is the closest to the truth a man can get," Johnny said.

"Even lemons seem sweet when they are hidden and forbidden, let alone lies. Do you think any human being is capable of love? Or is it only craving masked in nobility?" Seymour chuckled.

"Love is just a word… and words are herds of letters used to persuade crowds that something matters."

Seymour reached for the gun. He struggled not to slide from the sofa to the floor. The bullet standing next to the barrel remained alone on the table.

"This is how it all started. With a revolving cylinder," he said.

"I don't remember if my gun had it or not," Johnny replied.

"Let it be a revolving cylinder," Seymour said. "It gives a gun nobility."

"A spinning chance there might be a next morning."

"And there might be not. The first frame will be on the revolving cylinder. An empty chamber. A bullet standing on the table next to it and a palm resting beside it. Then a frame on the face. A man is brooding. Deep in thought, his grim gaze travels over everything. Then his hand lifts the bullet and puts it in the chamber. He spins the cylinder. Puts the barrel into his mouth and pulls the trigger," Seymour explained.

"I love it," Johnny said.

Max strode into the trailer. "Hi, guys! What are you doing?"

"And there he is. God of the weapons. A youngling in charge of the movie armory! Where were you last night?" Seymour said, pointing the gun at Max.

"I was with Nelly. Do you like the gun?" he asked, sitting on the table.

"It's outstanding," Seymour replied.

"I quarreled with the seller for two hours. And then stripped it in front of the Terminator crew," Max said.

Seymour opened the barrel to find it full of bullets. Only one hole was empty.

"That blank looks so real," Max noticed, looking at the bullet on the table. He took it between his fingers and squinted. "Oh my God… It looks precisely like the real bullet…"

"It should look like that. I got it especially for this occasion."

"Where did you get it?" Max was astonished.

Seymour didn't reply. He spun the cylinder and pulled the trigger. Max smiled.

"Against the odds," Seymour said.

"I think the barrel is set to spin on that chamber," Max said.

"Listen… About Nelly…"

"She told me that she is a whore you paid to get me laid." Silence settled on everyone.

Max was the one to break it. "Don't worry. I am okay with it. It is what it is. It would be a shame not to make good use of the benefit of having a rich uncle. I am going to enjoy it instead."

"I see the two of you were hanging out a lot," Seymour said, hitting the writer with his elbow.

"We do," Max said.

"Good. Your vocabulary is going to grow. It will make you more charming and your love life might not have to always depend on your uncle's pockets," Seymour said. "Go out and check if everyone has arrived. They have until midnight."

Max jumped to his feet.

"The bullet!" Seymour yelled.

Max turned and threw him the bullet. Then he rushed through the door.

"Wanna try it?" Seymour pushed the gun toward Johnny.

"Not really," he replied.

"Suit yourself," Seymour muttered.

"All right…" Johnny relented. "One last time…"

Seymour gave him the gun.

"Will it hurt me if it fires?" Johnny asked.

"You will have a sore throat," the midget replied.

Seymour smiled. Johnny span the cylinder, pushed the barrel in his mouth, and pulled the trigger. The sound of clicking echoed. "What are the chances? An empty chamber two times in a row?" Johnny said.

"You are a natural," Seymour murmured.

"Emanuel will do great," Johnny said.

The door opened and Max peeked in. "Everyone is here…"

Johnny stood and went towards the exit. When he reached the door, he stopped to look at Seymour. The midget was pushing the bullet into the last empty chamber.

"I will be there in a minute," he said.

Johnny went out. A dog started barking like crazy, running between people, cameras, and chairs around the trailer. Actors, makeup artists, cameramen, and other members of the crew were looking at Johnny as if expecting him to say something.

"He will come in a minute," Johnny said.

"He always does it," Max added. "He likes to be alone on the set before the shooting starts."

The pretty actress who got the role of Joana was lying in a chair with her legs over one handle, her soles dangling above the ground. Preparing to become Johnny, Emanuel was standing next to her, sliding his fingers over her soles. The dog was whimpering. He ran to the trailer and started clawing at the door with his paws.

Johnny felt the cold in his gut. "What did you mean when you said that the bullet looks real?"

"Well, blanks have crimped ends while real bullets look exactly like the one my uncle was holding," Max said. "It doesn't look like a regular blank."

The dog made a sound like a baby crying. Johnny blanched. His thoughts were insane while he begged the god of bullets to spare him the tragedy. Had he come now to take what the bullet didn't when the gun backfired? Johnny wondered as he kept begging the god of bullets to have mercy.

"Don't take this away from me!" Johnny mumbled, seeing Seymour dead and the filming sliding away, just like that. The dog was whimpering as if they were taking him to a slaughterhouse. Johnny hurried towards the door, forcing himself not to run. In that moment, he realized that talking to the god of bullets meant that he was very near a panic attack. He would not let himself surrender to his anxieties and present himself as a psycho in front of the entire crew. Just before his hand fell on the handle, a shot echoed. Johnny froze. His entire body went numb. He lost track of time. The trailer door opened.

Seymour clumsily put his foot on the little stair and coughed a few times. "These big bullets explode like crazy. I hope they killed all of Mia's shit in my throat. What's wrong? Why are you all looking at me like that?"

"I…"

Seymour burst out laughing. "You thought that was a real bullet in the gun?" He shouted as loud as he could to make sure every crew member heard him. "Not likely."

Seymour stood in front of everyone. "May I have your attention, please?" His roar made them fall silent. "I want to hit big with this movie! That means all of you must hit big. It means I will tolerate nothing but perfection. From now on, I will call actors by the name of their characters, as will every other member of the crew! Did I make myself clear?"

"Yes!" they cheered as one.

"Max, go fetch another bullet! Johnny and Joana, get your asses into the trailer!" Seymour yelled.

Max ran behind the crowd. Joana was barefoot. When they got inside, her soles were dirty. The writer took wet wipes to clean them. Emanuel sat on the sofa and leaned towards the table, his hands beside the gun. The cameramen checked their equipment. Seymour pulled another big bullet from his pocket and placed it on the table. The filming of the first frame was nearing.

To Johnny, it seemed funny, in a way. All these cameras, people, chairs, little ladders, lights, and other mechanisms encircling that small space… And one man, sitting on the sofa, pretending that all that around him doesn't exist.

"Before we even start, I want to tell you it will not be good," Seymour said to Emanuel.

"Please, always tell me. I want to improve," Emanuel replied.

"No! You should not want to improve!" Seymour hissed. "You should want to be somebody else. To act well, you need to switch the truths. Who is the best actor ever?"

"Ah… Antony Hopkins?"

"Wrong!" Seymour roared. "It's death. Nothing can out act death acting life. Pretending there is nothing but the current moment and the breath we are taking. Death has persuaded itself it is alive and even made her fear itself," Seymour explained. "And it did that because it was bored. Bored with peace. Life is merely a disturbance in death, which built a stage to act something fun. And that fun has turned into a loaded gun that will fire."

Emanuel was nodding. Johnny wondered if the poor guy had any idea what Seymour was talking about. He looked so lost. Yet a man intending to take his own life should look exactly like that.

"You must not look only grim. But grim and tired at the same time. Exhausted by the torment you want to end," Seymour continued.

"I understand," Emanuel said.

"You must look as if you have acknowledged that everything you see is death's face. You must know death is immortal and hope it will bring you permanent salvation. Yet you must feel pain for having to walk away from the pleasures this life could offer you…"

Emanuel closed his eyes.

"Think of all the plates you will have to wash if you fail. Imagine you have already failed and decided to punish yourself for not being good enough and to charge on life itself for not respecting you and creating you so small, worthless, and miserable." Seymour wouldn't stop. "But remain proud. There is no bigger chivalry than to charge on life itself."

When Emanuel opened his eyes, he was another person. Johnny felt as if he was looking at himself.

…

"Action!" Seymour shouted.

The writer took the gun from the table. There was one empty chamber. He looked at that hollow of hope for a few moments. Then he filled it with the last bullet standing on the table. The dog was barking outside. The writer span the cylinder, pushed the barrel in his mouth, and pulled the trigger. Everyone heard it fire. The silence prevailed.

"Oh, fuck!" someone muttered.

Emanuel was covered in blood. The dog was barking and jumping all over the trailer.

"Cut!" Seymour shouted.

EPILOGUE

Almost two years had passed since shooting the first frame. The actors and scriptwriters were gathered in a filming for a TV show. Laughing, they recalled how a light bulb had exploded at the same moment as Emanuel had pulled the trigger during their first attempt to shoot the first frame. How the dog, spooked, had rushed in and bit the poor actor's wrist. His vein exploded. Blood everywhere. Emanuel was lucky to be alive. And nobody could explain why the dog went insane or was even on set to begin with.

The star of the evening was running late. Johnny was so enchanted with his new white Ferrari that he missed the turn off three times. He was now a big name in the movie industry. That meant running late was a luxury he could afford. The movie had shaken the box office like an earth-quake. Multiple sex scandals with prostitutes had only made him even more famous.

When he finally arrived, Seymour was announcing their next movie together. Neither of them wanted to give any hints, but they agreed it was going to be something never seen before.

As they spoke, the big screens all around the studio played scenes from the 'Writer's Inferno: Heaven for Everyone.' Indra and Dominic were lying on the top of the hill, gazing at the sky, the white ocean foam murmuring on the rocks under the cliffs below. The sun was cradling their embraced bodies while the wind was pushing a little white cloud to the west.

Then the frame switched to a guy in white robes jumping in front of the writer and swallowing the intended bullet with his belly. As he fell dying, he pulled a letter from his robe and asked Johnny to deliver it to the church. The cameras clearly captured the address on the envelope (Sir Johnathan Street 777).

Then the scene switched to the trailer. The writer put the gun in his mouth and pulled the trigger. The people in the studio might have heard it fire before their screens went to black.

AUTHOR BIO

The identity of Mr. W. is yet to be revealed. He could be anyone, although the content of his books makes it hard to believe that he lives a family life with a wife and kids. His life moto is "Going insane is the most rational way of coping with reality."

Mr. W. is the author of "Long Live Hoes" originally published as "Stories from the Brothel" under Pink Flamingo Media. The book reached the finals for the Pauline Reagie Award.

He is also the author of "Google Diaries: Goodbye Letter." It is one of few parodies about artificial intelligence in which Google decides to commit suicide after encountering an article it cannot digest.

To make the package complete, he authored "Foot Fetish Manual: How to Tell Your Girlfriend You Would Like to Kiss Her Feet".

He likes chocolate, movies, and brothels.

The last affection he explains with his favourite quote, "If brothels were churches we would have orgies instead of wars. Guess what I like better."

Printed in Great Britain
by Amazon

43670434R00091